THE ROAD TOGETHER

A CONTEMPORANEOUS DRAMA IN FOUR ACTS

BY

GEORGE MIDDLETON

NEW YORK

HENRY HOLT AND COMPANY

1916

THE QUINN & BODEN CO. PRESS
RAHWAY, N. J.

To

SCUDDER AND LUCILE

Who have just started on the road together

PREFACE

THE spiritual level which any marriage achieves depends largely upon the quality of those who make it. Whatever its social import, of which few are deliberately conscious, it is essentially an affair of individuals. As they are and as they react to each other, so will the marriage be. Since it is only in marriage that society offers free and complete expression between them, it is there that the individual man and woman are most tested, most realized, and most offended.

If one considers the strangeness of sex—with its vagrancy and variation—and the tremulous psychic inheritances which uncontrollably veer our acts and emotions, one can only have deep charity when marriage ends in disillusion, and infinite wonder when it reaches rich fulfilment. Yet marriage endures somehow between these two extremes. Its bonds are obvious when based upon religious conviction, the responsibilities of children, the fear of admitting failure, and the pressure of convention. But the subtle and powerful bond, I believe, is that which is made by the daily habit of living together.

It is, in some way, to picture the strength of this latter bond when opposed to the vagrant claim of sex, that this present study of a group of individuals is dedicated. The resolution they attain is neither better nor worse than lies within their individual capacities and limitations. I am not concerned with any criticism of what that spiritual level may be. My object is to interpret their characters and the manner in which they finally realize themselves through the revelation of their self-deceptions under the contingencies of circumstance.   G. M.

June 1, 1916.

THE ROAD TOGETHER

THE PEOPLE CONCERNED

WALLACE KENT, *the District Attorney.*
DORA, *his wife.*
JULIA DEERING, *a novelist.*
TOM PORTER, *a retired banker, their intimate friend.*
FRED SAFFORD, *formerly cashier in Porter's bank.*
ARMOR DEERING, *Julia's brother; Kent's assistant.*
GEORGE GILMORE, *a Wall Street operator.*
WOODS, *a butler at the Kents'.*
MAID, *for Julia.*

A Waitress and two men—BIDDLE and TAINTER, friends of GILMORE—in ACT I. (These three have no dialogue.)

SCENES

THE FIRST ACT
At the KENTS'. *Early afternoon.*

THE SECOND ACT
The same. Late the next afternoon.

THE THIRD ACT
JULIA DEERING'S *Study. The same evening.*

THE FOURTH ACT
At the KENTS'. *Morning, ten days later.*

The action of the play takes place, at present, in a large Eastern city.

THE FIRST ACT

THE FIRST ACT *

The scene is a sort of informal reception room at the KENTS'. *Its furnishings are few but fine, intimating quiet extravagance. The general tone is soft green with a subtle suggestion that the room has been lived in a long while. There are folding-doors in back, which, when open, disclose the dining-room beyond. A small door in the left, at back, opens out on the hall, which apparently leads to the library beyond. The general entrance for callers, opening on this same hall, is down stage. Directly opposite this, on the right, is a deep bay-window daintily curtained. A grand piano, with its key-board towards the window, rests in the alcove thus made. At the foot of the piano stands a lovely Japanese screen, which, with several tall artificial palms, half shuts off part of the room, in an intimate cozy-corner effect. A desk-telephone upon a small table between the doors, a deep couch near the center, and some casually placed chairs complete the furnishing. The warm sun of an early spring afternoon pours in the window and dining-room in back.*

When the curtain slowly rises the folding doors are open disclosing KENT, GILMORE, *and two other men—* BIDDLE *and* TAINTER—*at the luncheon table. They are obviously absorbed in a conference, though they are*

* See copyright notice on back of title page.

7

not heard. A maid waits upon them. There is a pause.

WOODS, *a quiet-mannered butler, about sixty, enters from back. He carries a vase filled with large American Beauties which he brings down into the room and places upon the piano. He then goes back and pulls the folding-doors together, thus cutting the men from view. He goes out the main door. There is another pause.* TOM PORTER *comes in, followed by* WOODS.

PORTER *is a genial, lovable man, verging on fifty, with hair noticeably turning gray. He is observing, acute, and keenly sympathetic. In spite of a persistent cheerfulness he suggests deep wells of feeling. He is obviously very much at home.*

PORTER

You don't know when Mrs. Kent will be back?

WOODS

Almost any time now, Mr. Porter. Mrs. Kent's lunching out.

PORTER
(*Looking at clock*)

Um. Two-thirty. I'll wait a few moments, Woods.

WOODS
(*Taking his hat and coat*)

Very good, sir. I'm sorry I can't tell Mr. Kent that you're here.

PORTER
(*Surprised*)

He's at home?

WOODS

Yes, sir. Mr. Kent telephoned unexpectedly after Mrs. Kent had gone. Three gentlemen are lunching with Mr. Kent, sir. (*Indicating dining-room in back*) He left word I wasn't to interrupt him under any circumstances.

PORTER

Don't bother him, of course. (*He lights a cigarette*) Political pot boiling, I suppose?

WOODS

Yes, sir.—Would you like to wait upstairs?

PORTER

No. I'll smoke a cigarette here and look over the paper.
(*The telephone rings and* WOODS *answers it.*)

WOODS

Hello. No, Miss Deering. (PORTER'S *face brightens*) Mrs. Kent has not come in yet. Yes, Miss Deering. I'll tell her.

PORTER

Hold the wire.

WOODS

Just a moment; Mr. Porter's here.

(WOODS *goes out with* PORTER'S *hat and over-
coat.*)

PORTER

(*At the 'phone*)

Hello, Julia. I just dropped in to see Dora. Yes;
she's coming right back. What's that? Got to see her
alone? Ah, you can't scare me off like that. Yes.
Come over. I'll tell Dora. Yes; I'll wait. (*More
tenderly*) Julia, I'll always wait. What's that? No,
Central, I'm sorry *that* wasn't meant for you.

(DORA KENT *enters.* PORTER *hangs up the
receiver and they greet each other affectionately
as old friends.*

DORA KENT, *in spite of her girlish figure, is
nearing thirty. Her obvious refinement gently
colors a latent sense of power. Her manner,
though never negative, is quiet, reserved, and a
trifle dependent. She wears a smart suit and
hat.*)

DORA

(*Good-naturedly*)

Tom: I caught you.

PORTER

Dora, dear.

DORA

You can't leave Julia a single moment, eh? Oh,
don't deny it; I heard you.

PORTER

Julia was 'phoning you and like the popular song: 'I happened to be there.'

DORA

(*As he helps her remove her coat*)

Does she want me to ring her?

PORTER

No: she's coming right around.

DORA

Good. I haven't seen her for ages. I suppose she's absorbed in her new novel.

PORTER

She's absorbed in something, I know. She says she has something to tell you—alone.

DORA

Tom; are congratulations in order at last?

PORTER

(*Embarrassed*)

Her and me? Not yet.

DORA

Nonsense. I never thought a banker who'd beaten Wall Street would fall before a woman's hesitation.

PORTER

(*With a comic sigh of despair*)

Wall Street's got a system: Julia's only got temperament.

DORA

' (*Playfully*)

Tom, exactly what *is* temperament?

PORTER

I never was much on genealogy; but I should say temperament was certainly descended from St. Vitus.

DORA

(*Laughing*)

Tom, a lovely woman like Julia oughtn't to be at large.

PORTER

That's why I'm trying to persuade her to marry me. But she's awfully stubborn.

DORA

Don't hurry her. She'll find herself. We all do in time. (*He looks at her enigmatically, as she buries her face in the flowers, deeply inhaling their fragrance*) Aren't they lovely? Treated myself.

PORTER

How you love flowers.

DORA

Yes; like Lady Teazle: when they're expensive.
(*She lifts the vase, and as she turns to put it in
the dining-room, she notices the folding-doors
are closed.*)

PORTER

Woods said Wallace had some men unexpectedly
to lunch.

DORA

Did he say who?

PORTER

Blessed if I know. But, remember, this is the political season.

DORA

(*As she presses the push-button on wall*)

Yes: the annual show of spring candidates, eh?
Goodness, I do hope the politicians haven't been bother-
ing Wallace again. I can see it's getting on his nerves:
so I get it. (*Smiling*) Take my advice, Tom: never be
the wife of a District Attorney, if you can help it.

PORTER

(*Laughing*)

All right, Dora; nor the wife of the next Governor,
either, eh?

(*He pats her arm playfully.*)

DORA

(*Casually, as* WOODS *enters*)

Woods, did Mr. Kent leave any word for me?

WOODS

No, Mrs. Kent. I don't think he expected you back so early.

DORA

Do you happen to know who are lunching with Mr. Kent?

WOODS

I believe it's Mr. Biddle, Mr. Tainter, and— (*Trying to recall*) Mr. Gil—

PORTER
(*Quickly*)

Gilmore?

WOODS

Yes, sir; that's the name.

PORTER

(*Turning away and concealing his surprise*) Mr. George Gilmore, um—

DORA

That's all, Woods. When they get to the cigars tell Mr. Kent I'm home.

PORTER

Better also tell Mr. Kent I'm here, too.

WOODS

Very good, sir.

(DORA *is arranging the flowers, transferring some to other vases. As* WOODS *goes out, she notices that* PORTER *is standing lost in thought.*)

DORA

What's the matter, Tom?

PORTER

That's Tainter from up state, isn't it?

DORA

I suppose so; but I don't recall Wallace ever met him before.

PORTER

Biddle and George Gilmore, Wall Street. (*Dubiously*) I don't like it, Dora. These fellows want something.

DORA

Certainly they do: they're in politics. But all they'll get from Wallace is some of Letty's real home cooking.

PORTER

Well, I'd be a bit suspicious of them if they hadn't come here so openly; particularly now that Wallace is being mentioned for Governor.

DORA

(*Confidently*)

Oh, he'll know how to handle them. And his record for his entire career will make them understand the sort of man he is.

PORTER

Of course, of course. (*He watches her a moment*) What a part of his career you've been.

DORA

We have no children, Tom; so all I've had to give has gone into that.

PORTER

You've made it together.

DORA

Yes: together. And I've been more a part of it than even he realizes, haven't I?

PORTER

(*Understanding*)

Much more. (*He goes to her*) And Fred Safford?

DORA

(*With a slight start, as her mood suddenly changes*)

Fred Safford? (*She pauses as he looks at her in question*) Why should you speak of him?

PORTER

We seldom have since you sent him away.

DORA

I thought you and Julia knew that I've never seen nor heard from Fred since.

PORTER

And you've never told Wallace any of the particulars?

DORA

What good would it have done to have told him anything? That's all over, Tom.

(*The doors in back open and* WALLACE KENT *enters, closing them after him. For a short interval the three men—*GILMORE, TAINTER, *and* BIDDLE—*are again seen at the table, discussing together.*

WALLACE KENT *is reserved, forty, with a fine face and pleasant personality. He suggests hidden force and passion, coupled with considerable sensitiveness and intuition. He is a man not easily read.*)

KENT

Dora, back so early?

DORA

(*As they kiss*)

Oh, it was a dreadful bore.

KENT

Hello, Tom: what's this? A self-appointed investigating committee?

DORA

(*Laughing*)

Goodness, no; but perhaps you could tell us the secret. I asked Woods who were with you. Is it about the governorship nomination?

KENT

Right, as usual.

PORTER

And a nomination this year means election sure.

KENT

So they say.

DORA

(*Good-naturedly*)

Wallace; Tom doesn't like your company.

PORTER

(*Protesting*)

Now, Dora; you're telling tales out of school.

KENT

(*Casually*)

We're only talking over the coming State convention.

DORA

And you're getting all shades of opinion, eh?

KENT

You see the political training she has had, Tom?

DORA

Tom thinks you ought to be careful.

KENT

Indeed?

PORTER

Well, I don't know much about politics, but it isn't
the oyster plants that shed the pearls.

DORA

I said you'd know how to handle them.

KENT

(*With a slight touch of asperity*)
I'm not a fool, Tom.

PORTER

(*Seeing the need of an explanation and going to him
with genuine affection*)
Wallace, I'm afraid I'm in bad. Don't think it's an
intrusion on the part of a stray bachelor; but we three
and Julia have been pretty close these years and—

KENT

(*Seeing him hesitate*)

Say it, Tom.

PORTER

Well, I'd hate to have you get that nomination unless it came right, and without any strings.

DORA

(*Half-reproachfully*)

Why, Tom.

KENT

Nothing's to be decided yet; but the nomination will come right or not at all.

PORTER

Don't misunderstand. I know the pressure that's being brought to bear on you to delay that C. N. Y. Railroad case.

DORA

Tom, you really must be reprimanded. The idea of even thinking *these* gentlemen have anything to do with that case.

KENT

Tom means the Railroad crowd would do most anything to *get* the prosecuting attorney, eh?

PORTER

And those fellows have a lot of friends. (*Taking his hand*) I just wanted to hear you say it was all right. Forgive me.

KENT

Oh, everybody's suspicious of public officials nowadays.

DORA

(*Proudly*)

I'm not, Wallace. (*He smiles as she continues in good spirits*) But we mustn't deprive these gentlemen of your moral influence.

PORTER

No, no; I'm sure they need it.

DORA

Tom will stay here with me, won't you? He's waiting for Julia.

KENT

You're always waiting for Julia.

PORTER

One of the things I do best.

DORA

(*Over near door*)

I think this is Julia now. Stay a second, Wallace, and say hello.

(DORA *goes out.*)

PORTER

Can you hear my heart jumping? I'll never need digitalis so long as Julia's in my life.

KENT

(*Trying to be casual*)

May a very unimportant District Attorney ask when it's coming off?

PORTER

Sh! It's such a secret even Julia doesn't know it.

KENT

Perhaps she feels a *novelist* shouldn't marry.

PORTER

She's not a real novelist; she has money.

(*They laugh as the two women outside are heard greeting each other with intermingled sentences.*)

And they both understand what they're saying.

(*They enter.* DORA *having her arm affectionately about* JULIA.

JULIA DEERING *is a contrast to* DORA. *She is also about thirty, but with an opulent personality, impulsive and rather emotional in speech and temperament, a bit assertive and seemingly independent. She is attractively gowned though with a faint suggestion of the unconventional.*

She halts suddenly on seeing KENT, *is slightly confused, but quickly recovers and goes to him.*)

JULIA

Wallace, this *is* unexpected.   I thought you were
downtown.

KENT

Sounds as though you've been trying to avoid me.

DORA

Yes: it's been two weeks since even I have seen you.

KENT

(*Indicating dining-room*)
And now I have some hungry men waiting.

DORA

You see he will bring politics into the home.

JULIA

I want to see Dora; so don't let me keep you.   But
I must thank you again for letting my big brother as-
sist you in that Railroad case.   I haven't told him yet,
as I promised.

KENT

(*Enigmatically*)
I'll be glad to give Armor this chance for your sake.

PORTER

(*To* DORA)
Isn't that just like Wallace?

DORA

When does it go to trial?

KENT

It's on the calendar next week.

PORTER

They certainly have delayed it.

JULIA

I'm so sorry I sha'n't be here to watch Armor perform. He's so eager and enthusiastic about everything.

DORA

Surely you're not going away?

JULIA

I'm afraid so. I'm sailing before then.
                    (*They are all surprised.*)

KENT

You're going abroad?

DORA

Why, Julia—no—?

JULIA

Yes; to Corfu.

DORA

Not while the war's still on?

JULIA

Oh, I guess it won't pay attention to me. (*Smiling*) I'm a pacifist, you know.

KENT

But, Julia, this is all unexpected, isn't it?

JULIA

(*Avoiding his glance*)

I've been thinking for some time it's best.

(*Throughout the following a subtle tenseness, beneath the surface talk, is obvious.*)

DORA

Well, I know there's no use trying to persuade you how foolish it is, when you once get a notion.

PORTER

You're going to stay long?

JULIA

(*Vaguely*)

Oh, a year or so this trip.

DORA

But you will be lonely there.

JULIA

(*Half light-heartedly*)

Oh, no; I have my work.

PORTER

(*With a sigh*)

The world is full of people who have gone away.

JULIA

(*To* PORTER)

But don't take it so terribly. There's no reason to be glum—all of you. Maybe, Tom, you will come and see me when the war's over.

PORTER

(*Whimsically*)

Shouldn't wonder if I went before.

DORA

You may have to charter a submarine to get there.

PORTER

Then I'm glad I retired from my bank and kept some of it.

KENT

You're going alone?

JULIA

To finish my novel. My publishers are getting impatient.

PORTER

(*Mock seriously*)

These restless women with missions and no husbands!

JULIA

But you see, Tom, I'm already wedded to my art.

PORTER

Can't we find a country where bigamy's permitted?

DORA

(*Laughing*)

How many husbands do you think a woman needs?

PORTER

Lord! I don't know. That's every woman's eternal mystery.

(*They laugh nervously to cover their varying emotions.*)

KENT

But you're not sailing right away?

JULIA

I've got to get my passports.

DORA

Had your photograph taken and all that?

JULIA

(*Laughing*)

Yes.

KENT

It seems to me you're taking chances, Julia.

DORA

Can't anything persuade you to stay?

JULIA

(*Significantly*)

Oh—something may turn up to keep me. (*Glancing covertly at* DORA) I'll know to-day.

KENT

(*Shaking her hand*)

I'll see you before you sail. If there's anything I can do, let me know.

DORA

(*Going back with him*)

Have you everything you wish, dear? (*He nods*) We won't disturb you here?

KENT

Couldn't hear a sound back there if I wanted to. Oh, Tom; after what Julia's told us, are you sure you don't need a cocktail?

PORTER

No, Wallace. I'm like the fellow who was asked by a musical hostess if he'd like a *sonata* before dinner and he said he'd had two on the way uptown.

(*They laugh as* DORA *opens the doors in back and stands there a second with* KENT. PORTER *looks strangely at* JULIA *who is apparently under some agitation.* DORA *closes the doors, comes down, then goes to* TOM, *shakes her head indicating how sorry she is for him. Then she takes up her coat.*)

DORA

I'll be down in a moment. I must take off my hat which won't come off by itself. (*Closer, on second thought*) Julia; what's the reason you're going away?

PORTER

She's afraid she'll spoil me if she stays and marries me.

DORA

Something *may* come up to keep you, you said. (*Laughing good-naturedly*) Well, I'll give you a few seconds, Tom, to find out what it is. (*Hesitating*) Was this what you really came around to tell me?

JULIA

Wait till you come back.

DORA

Tom! Julia! You can't deceive me, you two. I'm afraid there is a conspiracy between you.

> (*She goes out, laughing.* JULIA *sinks into a chair as though she has scarcely been able to control herself. She obviously waits till* DORA *has gone.*)

JULIA

Tom! (*He comes to her*) Fred Safford has come back.

PORTER
(*Astonished*)

Safford!

JULIA

Yes. He's in town.

PORTER

You've seen him?

JULIA

No. He 'phoned. He's been here several weeks. He's coming to see Dora this afternoon.

PORTER
(*Hardly able to grasp it*)

To see Dora!

JULIA

Yes. He probably thought Wallace was downtown. I tried to get him to see me first; but he wouldn't. He seemed desperate, as though he'd been drinking or something.

PORTER
(Realizing)

Good God! She mustn't see him.

JULIA

Why not?

PORTER
(Surprised)

You ask me that?

JULIA

He says he has a right to see her.

PORTER
(Emphatically)

He no longer has any rights here.

JULIA

He thinks he has: he still loves her.

PORTER
(Dismissing it)

But all that is over with *her*.

JULIA

Are you sure?

PORTER

Certainly. (*Between his teeth*) The dirty pup, to come back.

JULIA
(*Surprised*)
You never said a thing like that about him before.

PORTER

I've had my reason for being silent about him. (*With a determined air*) What's his address?

JULIA

He didn't tell me.

PORTER

That's like him. But I'll find him.

JULIA

No; you mustn't stop him from seeing her.

PORTER
(*Astonished*)
I mustn't!

JULIA
(*Realizing the difficulty of her position*)
Wouldn't it be best if—if she found out for sure how she really felt?

PORTER

(*Persistently*)

But I tell you it's all over, as far as *she* is concerned.

JULIA

It was mighty important—*once*.

PORTER

Yes; of course, it was. When she and Wallace weren't hitting it off. (*Dismissing it*) That was only the usual let down after a few years of married life.

JULIA

But you seem to keep forgetting that Fred *had* come into her life; that she loved him.

PORTER

No; I'm not. And she did what she should have done; she sent him away; she thought of Wallace—his career and—

JULIA

And not of Fred.

PORTER

Wallace loved her. He still loves her. You know that. (JULIA *turns away*) Why, Julia, you're her very best friend; surely, *you* wouldn't want anything to come between her and Wallace?

JULIA

(*Quickly*)

Then you, too, are not sure of how she may still feel toward Fred?

PORTER

I'm sure she mustn't see him.

JULIA

You'll prevent it?

PORTER

If I can.

JULIA

(*Desperately*)

Tom; you—you *mustn't* interfere.

PORTER

(*Surprised and incredulous*)

Julia!

JULIA

I have my reasons.   I can't explain to you.

PORTER

(*Hurt*)

Can't explain to *me!*

JULIA

Let me see Dora alone and she can decide.

PORTER

Julia, your word has always been law to me.

JULIA

Then please do as I ask. Don't—don't interfere.

PORTER

(*After a pause, not understanding*)

Very well; if you say so.

JULIA

Tom—

PORTER

Perhaps you women see best. If she is *willing* to see him I won't interfere. (*With quiet determination*) But if he tries to force himself upon her against her wish, I know a way to silence Fred Safford.

(DORA *has come in and heard the last few words. They turn embarrassed as she slowly comes down and speaks very quietly.*)

DORA

Tom, you've been speaking again about Fred? Has anything happened to him? Is he—?

JULIA

He's come back.

DORA

Here? (JULIA *nods*) Tom, is this true?

PORTER

Julia has just told me.

DORA

(*As though not understanding*)

But he promised—

JULIA

(*Abruptly*)

He still loves you.

DORA

He still loves me?—Too bad! Too bad! I had
hoped he would forget.
>   (*She goes to chair and sits down. PORTER lays*
>   *his hand in appeal on JULIA's arm as though*
>   *asking silence. Suddenly DORA turns abruptly.*)
I understand now. He wants to see me.

JULIA

Yes, he's coming here today.

PORTER

Unless—

DORA

(*Startled*)

No, no. He mustn't come here. (*Glancing back*
where KENT is) I sha'n't see him.

JULIA

(*In spite of* TOM'S *protest*)

Then at my place.

PORTER

Julia!

JULIA

(*To* PORTER)

Please leave me alone with Dora.

PORTER

(*After looking at* JULIA *and resigned to the situation*)
All right. Remember, I'm just around the corner,
if you need me. I'll 'phone you later, Julia. Bye-bye,
Dora. Let me know what you decide. (*Under his
breath as he goes out*) The pup—

(DORA *has moved her hand across her brow in a
bewildered fashion, not noticing his last words.*
PORTER *has gone out.* JULIA *makes sure the
door is closed after him. She stands looking at*
DORA *for a moment. Then she goes to* DORA
*and puts her hand affectionately on her
shoulder.*)

JULIA

(*Tenderly*)

You still love Fred?

DORA

(*Indefinitely*)

Oh, Julia, don't!

JULIA

See him. I'll arrange it: at my place. No one
need—

DORA

No; *not* if he still loves me.

JULIA
(*Moving away slightly*)]
You aren't afraid, are you?

DORA

Why go over it again? What good will it do?

JULIA

But hasn't he meant something to you?

DORA

Yes. It would mean something to *any* woman when
a man accepts a decision as bravely as he did. I've not
forgotten. I've been grateful. But I thought Fred
knew it was final.

JULIA

But you'll never be sure of your *own* feeling till you
see him again.

DORA
(*Slowly as though puzzled*)
Why do *you* wish me to be sure of my own feeling?

JULIA

(*With growing agitation*)

I'd like you to be happy.

DORA

But I am—I am—as far as I can be.

JULIA

Then you do fear to see Fred.

DORA

No; I don't fear to see him; but it must stay as it
is between us—for his own sake.

JULIA

You *also* forget Fred loves you.

DORA

I'm sorry, sorry.

JULIA

Isn't love everything?

DORA

No; not everything.

JULIA

It should be in marriage.

DORA

(*Looking at her*)

You are reproaching me!

JULIA

I've *said* nothing to make you feel that.

DORA

No, not in words: but I feel your silent reproach, just as I felt it when I sent him away. You've always thought I should have gone with him.

JULIA

Only because I didn't want any one to be cheated.

DORA

Fred may have been cheated; but it was the situation not I that made it hard for him. I did what was right by Wallace.

JULIA

Did you?

DORA

(*Confidently*)

Oh, yes. He needed *me*. A scandal would have hurt his work—his political career. What he has become through me is sufficient proof I did the right thing.

JULIA

(*Turning away*)

Success is not always a proof of what is right.

DORA

It's my justification for any wrong I may have done Fred. (*Going to her*) But, Julia; why do *you* insist on my seeing him again? (JULIA *is silent*) We've been so close ever since we were children; we've shared all our confidences. But you've come here now to urge something my whole instinct rebels at. I think I've the right to ask you for an answer.

JULIA

I've told you.

DORA

No. You haven't explained your reason for wanting it.

JULIA

I can't explain.

DORA

There must be something more than your consideration of me back of this. There's some reason vital to *you*.

JULIA

No. I—

DORA

(*Her intuitions now thoroughly alert*)

You didn't want any one cheated, you said. You weren't thinking *only* of Fred.

JULIA

Dora, I've put myself in a false position.

DORA

Has *this* anything to do with your reason for going away? (*There is a pause*) Julia—has it?

JULIA

Yes.

DORA

Something might persuade you to stay. It *is* something to do with me. Have I done you any wrong? Have I cheated *you* in any way?

JULIA

(*Seeing she must face it*)

I—I might at least have had a *chance* for happiness, if you had—

DORA

(*Quickly*)

If I had—what?

JULIA

Oh, all that's worst in me is coming out. Please, please, let's stop.

DORA

(*Insistently*)

If I had what?

JULIA

(*Almost inaudibly*)

If—if you had gone with Fred.

DORA

(*Looking at her in astonishment and stepping back*)

Julia!

JULIA

(*Defensively*)

Well, haven't you been living a lie here?

DORA

No!

JULIA

Yes, you have. You've loved one man and lived with another.

DORA

(*Scarcely believing what she has heard*)

Julia, Julia, I see it now. *I* was in the way. I am still in the way. That's *why* you wanted me to go with Fred; why you wish it even now!

JULIA

(*Quickly*)

Not go with him now unless you love him; only give yourself the test.

DORA

(*Gazing incredulously at her*)

Julia! Don't turn from me. You mean you love Wallace?

(JULIA *tries to meet her gaze, then she turns and bows her head in silent acknowledgment of the truth. DORA looks at her a long while, then impulsively goes to her, clutching her arm.*)

Does Wallace know this?

JULIA

No. He loves you.

DORA

(*Releasing her hold, convinced*)

Yes. He loves me.

JULIA

I've been unkind to him. I've even led him to believe it was Tom. (*Earnestly*) You know I've never been disloyal to you.

DORA

Yes; I'm sure of that. (*Still incredulous*) You love him. That explains much I never understood. Poor Julia!

JULIA

You pity me?

DORA

No; I just understand.

JULIA

(*Passionately*)

But I tell you, Dora, if Wallace *had* loved me I wouldn't have been the coward—

DORA

That I was? (*Eyeing her*) I wonder. I wonder.

JULIA

(*Humbled*)

Oh, forgive me, dear. I'm all impulse and selfishness. I've suffered a lot. It broke my defenses just now unexpectedly seeing Wallace and knowing I was going away. That's why I'm going. I can't stand it. I—forgive me.

DORA

(*Very tenderly, after a pause*)

It's best you go, for a while.

JULIA

Yes. (*As though thoroughly ashamed of herself*) But this won't make a mess between you and me?

DORA

No. I haven't forgotten all you did for me—once.

JULIA

I don't know what got into me.   It was just the wild chance that perhaps—

DORA

I'm not angry; only hurt a little somehow.

JULIA

You ought never to speak to me again.

DORA

(*Tenderly*)

Love makes us all do foolish things.   There, there, Julia; let's say no more about it.

JULIA

(*After a pause*)

And Fred?

DORA

(*Going to button and pushing it*)

I sha'n't see him.

JULIA

You're right.   It's better all around.   *I'll* tell him.

DORA

(*Calmly*)

No; I'll write him and you will see that he gets the letter.

JULIA

I'll ask him to go away.

DORA

Yes; and tell him to be a *man*. (Woods *enters.*)
Woods, if a Mr. *Safford* should call—

WOODS

I was just going to announce him.

JULIA

(*Tense*)

But—

(FRED SAFFORD *enters quickly. They all stand
still and silent.*

SAFFORD *is almost the wreck of what was
once a strong, handsome man; his face is worn
and dissipated, mouth hard and fingers nervous.
He is thirty-eight but looks older. There is a
very slight suggestion he has been drinking
which tends to let down whatever reserve may
have been left. There is only an occasional
flash of what must have been an old charm.*)

WOODS

(*After a slight pause*)

Anything further, Mrs. Kent?

JULIA

(*Relieving the situation*)

Will you see if my car is there.

WOODS

Certainly.

(*They wait till* WOODS *goes out.*)

JULIA

(*Goes to* SAFFORD)

Hadn't you better come with me? (SAFFORD *motions her aside*) How you've changed, Fred! (*Looks at him quite a while, half shrinking*) Dora, say goodbye to Wallace. I don't want to interrupt his luncheon with those gentlemen.

(*Saying this for* SAFFORD *to know* KENT *is in the next room.* SAFFORD *is surprised at this, but apparently accepts it.*)

Be careful, Fred, be careful!

(DORA *has stood as one transfixed. She has not taken her eyes off* SAFFORD, *who is also staring at her.* JULIA *goes out closing the door.*

There is a pause: SAFFORD *takes a few steps nearer to her, hesitates, then slowly goes to her, as if to embrace her. She instinctively puts her arms between them, pushes him back, breaking from him and silencing him. He halts, half in query. They play the whole scene with a quiet intensity as though afraid of an impending interruption from* KENT.)

DORA

What do you mean by coming here?

SAFFORD

I thought you'd be alone.

DORA

But why did you break your promise?

SAFFORD

(*Surprised*)

You don't want to see me at all?

DORA

I didn't say that.

SAFFORD

You women don't have to *say* things.

DORA

(*More tenderly*)

Oh, why did you come back, Fred?

SAFFORD

Didn't you ever think I would?

DORA

I thought your promise was sufficient.

SAFFORD

I was a fool to make it.

DORA

Even when I asked it?

SAFFORD

It cheated us out of our happiness.

DORA

(*Hurt more and more throughout*)

Would it have been happiness?

SAFFORD

Beginning to doubt?

DORA

(*Looking at him*)

No, Fred. I'm sorry; but seeing you again, I know it couldn't have been happiness.—How you have changed!

SAFFORD

(*Tensely*)

Not in my love for you.

DORA

Hush!

SAFFORD

Dora!

DORA

(*Repressed*)

Don't, my husband! Oh, let me think—please, please.

SAFFORD

I gave you time to think once, and I lost you.

DORA

(*On the defensive*)

You never had me. I see it now, never!

SAFFORD

(*Forcibly*)

Yes; I did.

DORA

No, no. I was down, weary, sick. Marriage wasn't what I thought and—

SAFFORD

You're not going to hand out that usual talk?

DORA

(*Breaking slightly*)

God, Fred! Don't you see I didn't want to regret? It kept me up: the knowledge that I'd done the wisest thing for us all.

SAFFORD

(*Emphatically*)

What you did to me made me what I am. Look at me.

DORA

(*Shuddering*)

No, no.

SAFFORD

Yes, look at me. (*Slowly*) I'm a disappointment, a failure, eh?

DORA

(*Moving from him*)

Yes; and it hurts.

SAFFORD

(*With a touch of genuine feeling*)

I would have been different if I'd had you.

DORA

(*Slowly shrinking from him with growing disillusionment*)

Oh, why didn't you forget me?

SAFFORD

As you did? I couldn't, Dora; I couldn't.

DORA

I never forgot you, Fred. I thought you were a strong man, strong in your love; strong enough to

make your love, if nothing else, keep you clean.   But
you've soiled yourself and me in coming back this way
—in being what you are.

SAFFORD

Did you ever once inquire about me?

DORA

I trusted you.

SAFFORD

Then, how do you know what I've become?

DORA

Oh, Fred, it's in your face.

SAFFORD

I love you, I tell you.

DORA

Love?

SAFFORD

Yes.   You've always been near me.   If I'd owned
you just once I might have forgotten.

DORA

Is that the way men like you forget?

SAFFORD

I've tried to forget you, but I couldn't.

DORA

I gave you credit for everything.

SAFFORD

Oh, no, you didn't. You really blamed me for going so easily.

DORA

No!

SAFFORD

Yes, you did. I know women. You'd have come with me, if I'd *made* you. (*She gazes incredulously*) But I couldn't stay and force you. You know Porter made me get out. Don't try to fool me.

DORA

(*Not understanding*)

Tom?

SAFFORD

I want you to forgive me for going. But he knew the hole I was in. I didn't intend to *keep* the money, but I was desperate—

DORA

You stole money? You left Tom's bank because—?

SAFFORD

(*Startled*)

Didn't he tell you?

DORA

(*Shrinking back*)

No! Never that!

SAFFORD

(*With a touch of bravado*)

Well, it makes no difference. You'd have to know some day. I was desperate *after* you threw me over—

DORA

(*Revolted*)

After! And I thought it was your strength that made you go!

SAFFORD

I tell you you've changed towards me because I didn't take you as a man should when he wants a woman. But I've come back for you now.

DORA

(*Sarcastically*)

How you love me!

SAFFORD

(*Pleading quickly*)

You've got to save me, Dora. Every time life shuffled me rotten cards, I knew I'd have played to win by your side. What was still decent in me reproached me and made me cling to the thought of you. I couldn't pull myself up alone. The loss of you kept you alive. My love for you made me go wrong first and you've got to help me to go back or I'm finished.

DORA
(*Incredulously staring at him*)
You blame me! You miserable—

SAFFORD
You'll blame yourself for what I am when you've thought it over. (*Reproachfully*) You clung to me when you needed me.

DORA
I was unhappy, I— (*Turning firmly as he sneers*) No. I won't make excuses. Perhaps I did you a wrong.

SAFFORD
(*Bitterly*)
But you found consolation with your husband.

DORA
(*Her face brightening*)
Yes.

SAFFORD
(*Sneering*)
And I suppose you *have* made yourself part of his career?

DORA

Yes, I have—as I told you I would. I've helped
to make him—

SAFFORD

What? A man respected and honest, eh?

DORA

Yes!

SAFFORD

(*Sneering*)

Honest?

DORA

What do you mean?

SAFFORD

Honest?

DORA

(*As he laughs bitterly*)
What do you think you'll gain by insulting him?

SAFFORD

(*Abruptly pointing to dining-room door*)
Who's your husband lunching with?

DORA

(*Involuntarily*)
Mr. Tainter—Mr. Gilmore and—   (*Suddenly*

realizing and becoming confused) How did you know they were here?

SAFFORD

Didn't you hear Julia tell me? But I didn't know *who* they were. Thanks for telling me. Gilmore, eh? *George* Gilmore! And Tainter, eh? I thought so.

DORA

(*Recalling* PORTER'S *suspicions, as* SAFFORD *laughs*) What do you mean?

SAFFORD

For three weeks since I came back, I've been nosing around. That's why I waited before I saw you. I was afraid you'd pull this good husband stuff. I've found out what I wanted to know about *him*. And I'll tell you *how* I found out if you want to know.

DORA

Leave this house!

SAFFORD

He's playing crooked politics.

DORA
(*Sharply*)

No.

SAFFORD

Watch that C. N. R. Railroad indictment. You'll find these fellows pressed for trial, like hell you will.

DORA

(*Defensively*)

These men have nothing to do with that case.

SAFFORD

Haven't they? Well, their friends have and these are the fellows who can give your husband what *he* wants—the nomination!

DORA

Leave this house!

SAFFORD

(*Pushing her gradually towards the window, step by step*)

Dora, Dora! Don't treat me this way. I'll do anything to get you. I love you. Come with me.

DORA

Go! Go!

SAFFORD

He's no justification for what you've done me.

DORA

Don't touch me. If you don't go, I'll call him and tell him you are a thief!

SAFFORD

I don't give a damn now. I won't live without you.

DORA

You've stripped everything. Go. Go! Sh!

(She has retreated slowly to window by piano. The doors open in back and KENT, *followed by* GILMORE, TAINTER, *and* BIDDLE *enter.* KENT *believes they are alone.*

GILMORE, *an impressive, authoritative man about fifty;* BIDDLE, *somewhat younger, is suave and polished;* TAINTER, *rather rough and important.*

DORA *instinctively covers* SAFFORD. *They are both hidden by the plants and flowers which screen the piano.* SAFFORD *grips her arm and listens with a sneer, as she stands dazed.)*

KENT

(Indicating)

We'll be more comfortable in the library.

GILMORE

(In a persuasive, confidential tone)

It's only a question of a few months, Kent; the reason for delaying the trial can *appear* perfectly legitimate, can't it, gentlemen? *(Other two agree)* Besides, your record protects you from criticism and our position guarantees your success. *(He sees* KENT'S *uncertainty)* But let's go over it again. Perhaps we can put our offer in a more attractive way. *(To others)* Fine mild Perfectos these.

(The others, at KENT'S *suggestion, go out*

towards the library. GILMORE *follows.*
WOODS *has appeared at the folding-doors.*
KENT *sees him.*)

KENT

Woods, did you telephone my assistant?

WOODS

Mr. Deering will be up later.

KENT

These gentlemen need not see him, understand?

WOODS

Yes, sir.

KENT

Serve liqueurs in the library.

WOODS

Yes, sir.
(KENT *goes thoughtfully towards the library.*
Murmur of men heard greeting him. WOODS
closes doors in back and cuts himself from view.
DORA *and* SAFFORD *are alone.*)

SAFFORD
(*Sneering*)

You see!

DORA

Go!

SAFFORD

I'm a thief, am I? Well, what's he?

DORA

(*Dazed*)

I don't believe it.

SAFFORD

He'll try to fool you.

DORA

(*Determined*)

I'll find out.

SAFFORD

(*With hope*)

And if—?

DORA.

(*Finally*)

Never with you. (*Motions toward main door*)
Go! Go! You're dead to me.

SAFFORD

(*Tensely*)

Dead, am I? Then you've wrecked me; you've
killed me for *his* career and he's crooked—*crooked.*

(*Bitterly*) Don't forget you've killed me and he's going crooked in spite of your sacrifice. Don't forget that.

DORA

(*Throughout*)

Go! Go! Go!—It isn't true!
> (*She half pushes him in disgust out of the room, closing the door. Then she staggers up to the folding-doors, leans against them, looking towards library where her husband is. But in spite of her words, her face is set in doubt and suspicion.*)

CURTAIN

THE SECOND ACT

THE SECOND ACT

Same as the first act. Late the next afternoon.
The curtain rises on DORA *seated at piano playing*
an aria from Madame Butterfly. She has on an after-
noon gown. She seems abstracted, pauses, and looks
impatiently out of window. She does this a second
time and apparently sees KENT. *She gives an eager*
cry, then crosses quickly to door as though to meet
him, but changes her mind and comes slowly into room.
Though she instinctively resents her own doubt, it is
seen that she feels she must question him about SAF-
FORD'S *accusation.*

KENT *comes in and throws aside hat and coat.*
There is a note of quiet determination in his manner.
He has some unopened letters in his hand which he
puts on table.

KENT

Hello, Dora. Feeling better?

DORA

Yes.

KENT

I came in too late last night to disturb you and I
thought you'd better sleep this morning. Has Armor
come yet?

DORA

He missed you yesterday. Didn't you see him at your office?

KENT

I haven't been there today. (*Looks at clock*) Have my brokers 'phoned?

DORA

Mr. Cooper did. He said he'd ring you up later. (*After a pause as though she half hesitates to take up the subject*) But you haven't told me about the luncheon yesterday.

KENT

There's nothing to tell.

DORA

(*As he is glancing through mail*)
You're still considering being a candidate?

KENT

For Governor? (*She assents slowly*) No; I decided not to run.

DORA

(*Obviously relieved, though surprised*)
Not to run?

KENT

Why, I thought you'd be disappointed?

DORA

(*With conflicting emotions*)

I am disappointed, if you are. We've both looked forward to it so. But I know there must have been good reasons why you have refused their support.

KENT

They offered it; but I couldn't accept their terms. (*She gives a sigh of relief which causes him to look at her somewhat puzzled*) Dora, aren't you feeling well?

DORA

I had a wretched night: I'll be better now.

KENT

Here's some mail for you.

DORA

(*As she takes up the letters, casually looking through them*)

Bridge? Belgium Relief. Wedding announcements?

KENT

Not Tom Porter's?

DORA

(*Good-naturedly*)

No.—Wallace, why haven't you been nice to Tom lately?

KENT

Nonsense.

DORA

No, you haven't. You've really been awfully touchy.
Here. (*Giving him some letters*) You'd better take
these.

KENT

(*Glancing at envelopes; tossing them aside unopened*)
Bills, I presume.

DORA

Haven't some of them been kept waiting quite a
time? The florist and——

KENT

(*Avoiding the subject*)
I'll attend to them later.

> (*She has kept several letters in her hand and
> now, on seeing one, which she recognizes is from
> SAFFORD, she starts; then obviously conceals it
> from KENT, who is still glancing through the
> rest of the mail.*)

They've reserved seats for Tristan. It's the last per-
formance.

DORA

Will you be able to go with me?

KENT

If I'm busy, get Tom.

DORA

Wagner always gives him a headache. He prefers Butterfly.

KENT

I suppose that mushy music suits his mood.

DORA

Still, he'll go, I know, if that important Railroad trial *is* taking all your attention.
                    (KENT *looks at her quickly.*)
                         (WOODS *enters.*)

WOODS

Mr. Deering.
          (KENT *assents and* WOODS *goes out, taking* KENT'S *hat and coat.*)

DORA

(Tentatively)

I'll go upstairs if it's private.

KENT

No, stay; of course, stay.
          (DORA *is pleased that he seems to wish her to remain. As* KENT *goes momentarily out to meet* DEERING, DORA *looks triumphantly at*

SAFFORD'S *letter which she has kept concealed in her hand.*)

DORA

I told you it wasn't so!

> (*She tears the unopened letter up, with a certain finality, as though her doubts were over. DEERING and KENT, who have been heard greeting outside door, enter.*
>
> *ARMOR DEERING, JULIA'S brother, has not yet reached thirty. He is virile, clean-cut, and ingratiating. He has an air of reliable manliness beneath his apparent earnestness, which, fortunately, is tempered by a sense of humor.*)

DEERING

How'd do, Mrs. Kent.

DORA

(*Greeting him*)

Sorry I missed you yesterday, Armor.

KENT

Cigarette?   Highball?

DEERING

(*Refusing both*)

No. You know I'm going to be married; so I'm reforming my present life.

Dora

(*Without any hidden intention*)
Then, Armor, you and Sally must be more than delighted at this opportunity Mr. Kent has given you.

Kent

What opportunity?

Dora

Why, the C. N. Y. case.

Deering

Sister Julia just told me you decided to let me help you handle it in court. I thought that was the reason you wished to see me here.

Dora

Why, of course. You spoke of it yesterday, Wallace, during luncheon.

Kent

Yes, yes; but— (*There is a momentary pause*) Well, Armor, you know I'd do whatever I could for you and Julia, but—

Deering

(*Sensing the situation*)
Don't let it embarrass you if Mrs. Kent or Julia misunderstood.

DORA

(*Puzzled*)

Wallace, I was sure you said——

KENT

(*Looking at her keenly*)

I think you are mistaken, dear.

DORA

Perhaps; yet——

(*She stops a second, puzzled; then as she turns she looks at the torn pieces of* SAFFORD'S *letter still in her hand, her suspicions again aroused. She takes flower vase, goes up into dining-room, throws letter in fireplace, removes the fading flowers from vase, etc., and is absorbed in thought, yet half unconsciously at times, look- ing in at the two men who speak in a quick, business-like fashion during this.*)

DEERING

I felt all along it's your case.   It will mean a lot to your political future.

KENT

I was not considering that.

DEERING

I don't believe you know all I've unearthed.   It will cause a political earthquake; accounts juggled;

lobby expenses to ward off strike bills; expenses toward political compaigns—all used out of funds, which, by right, belong to the stockholders.

KENT

(*Feeling his way throughout*)

Perhaps, after all, you are better acquainted with the case. But are the facts you have unearthed admissible as evidence under the indictment?

DEERING

I'm not absolutely positive, sir.

KENT

But that's vital.

DEERING

I know a mere hint of what I've got will lead the Governor to make an investigation of this whole situation.

KENT

You advise me to make political capital out of this?

DEERING

(*Smiling*)

It's always good to have it up your sleeve if you have to take your coat off.

KENT

(*Casually*)

It's on the calendar for next Monday, isn't it?

DEERING

Yes, sir.

KENT

I could hardly go through all the evidence before then, could I?

DEERING

(*Eagerly*)

I'm well enough prepared to open.

KENT

(*Hesitating*)

From what you say this appears such an important case that—

DEERING

You feel you'd better handle it entirely yourself?

KENT

(*Frankly*)

What would you advise in my place?

DEERING

(*Smiling*)

You've had more experience with crooks than I've had; but, then, I'm still young.

KENT

I can probably get to the bottom in a few days. I understand their counsel has asked for a postponement and if we agree——

DEERING

(*Quickly*)

I'd advise against having this put over. Their counsel has already exhausted every technicality to keep this out of court. The court would allow further postponement only upon *our* motion and that wouldn't be wise.

KENT

Still, I hardly believe it advisable to spoil our case by pushing it prematurely.

DEERING

But there's no doubt about their guilt.

KENT

Unfortunately moral certainty is not legal proof. If this case should be thrown out on a technicality, it means immunity from future prosecution.

DEERING

(*Emphatically*)

Their object is to keep it off the Spring calendar so that, after the Summer recess, the case may be tried before another Judge; and they would gain the usual benefits of delay. Besides, next Fall, with the muddle

of Municipal and State elections, they figure on the
people being blinded to the real situation should *all*
the facts be disclosed. And the yellow papers are
already beginning to ask questions. So I don't believe
you'll be able to explain satisfactorily to the voters
why you've put off this case, after I've forced it to
trial, should you, by any chance, expect to rely on
their votes in the coming election.

Kent

(*Forcibly*)

I don't need the people's votes; I won't be turned
from any course I think is right. If I halt this case
one month or two—over to the Fall even—it will be
because I think it wise.

Deering

I beg your pardon if I seemed outspoken. But I
felt sure of my position.

Kent

I'm not intending to *dismiss* the case.

Deering

I can't help thinking how embarrassing it might
prove for you if you delayed this prosecution too long,
and the people should ask *why*.
>   (*As* Dora *has come down placing the empty
>   flower vase on the piano, she catches the drift*

*of the last few speeches. She stands listening
intently, unobserved by* KENT.)

KENT

Why attempt to explain anything to the people?

DEERING

(*With feeling*)

Mr. Kent; I'm deeply grateful for all you've done
for me. I know I'd never been appointed your assistant if I hadn't happened to be Julia's brother.
I'm afraid I presumed on that friendship. You know
best about this, sir. You must excuse me if——

KENT

(*He is obviously moved. His manner is affectionate
and it is seen his course has been difficult*)
Armor, Armor. Forgive me. I quite appreciate
the disappointment this must be to you.

DEERING

(*Good-naturedly*)

Truck! I saw a halo sprouting on my head.

KENT

I understand. But you're exaggerating, you're over-
zealous; it's only a temporary delay and it seems most
expedient. Come, come. Aren't we both overdoing its
importance a little? (*They laugh*) There'll be other
things that'll come your way soon.

DEERING

Sure: I'm going to get married.

(WOODS *enters.*)

WOODS

Mr. Porter.

DORA

All right, Woods.

(KENT *turns and sees* DORA *standing there.* WOODS *goes out.*)

DEERING

(*Noting there is some embarrassment as they gaze at each other*)

Excuse me for a moment, Mrs. Kent; Sister Julia is in the car with Tom Porter, I think. I'll tell her I'm here.

(DEERING *goes out.*)

DORA

Why?

KENT

What?

DORA

This delay?

KENT

You heard what I said.

DORA

That's not the real reason. Something at luncheon yesterday——

KENT

Bosh, dear!

DORA

If not for the Governorship nomination, why?

KENT

What makes you suspect anything?

DORA

My instinct.

KENT

You women have many false instincts.

DORA

They are as real to us as facts.

KENT

(*Plausibly*)

Dear, why have you suddenly grown suspicious? It's not like you.

DORA

No, it's not; yet if one suddenly doubts what one has trusted?

KENT

Don't you trust me?

DORA

(*With impulsive emphasis as though to reassure her-self*)

Yes, I do—I do—of course, I do. (*He pats her arm;*
then she smiles as though she were ashamed of her
doubt) I was a bit puzzled. That's all.

(*Enter* PORTER.)

PORTER

(*Cheerfully, seeing them together*)

Ah! pretty picture! Not interrupting, am I?

DORA

(*Lightly*)

You're a habit; never an interruption.

PORTER

Glad I'm something you can't lose.

DORA

But where's Julia? I thought Armor said she was
with you?

PORTER

She's waiting outside in the car for me. Said she'd
promised to pick Armor up, too. I tried to get her to
come in with me; but I can't do anything with her.

She's in one of her moods. It pays to be a writer; everybody excuses them when they're flighty.

DORA

You try to persuade her, Wallace. Perhaps she'll have some tea. (*Quietly to him as he is near door*) And besides, you'd better explain to her about Armor. (KENT *goes out.* PORTER *turns as* DORA *comes close to him*) Tom?

PORTER

Yes, Dora.

DORA

How was it Fred wasn't arrested?

PORTER

(*Surprised*)

Arrested?

DORA

Yes; for his theft at the bank.

PORTER

He told you?

DORA

Yes. He thought I knew. He said you had discovered it. Did any one else know?

PORTER

Fortunately not.

DORA

Then the money was restored?

PORTER

Yes—in full. (*Not quite understanding her mood*) But don't worry.

DORA

(*Interrupting*)

Did he restore it? (PORTER *smiles cynically in spite of himself; she steps nearer to him, grasping the situation*) You—you put it back!

PORTER

(*Deprecating it*)

Now don't let's talk of that.

DORA

What a friend you have been—what a friend!

PORTER

(*Patting the hand which she has put in his*) I'd do anything for you and Julia.

DORA

Then why didn't you tell me of this before?

PORTER

(*Half whimsically*)

Dora, we all need illusions to help us over the hard places.

DORA

No—no, we don't. They make us sentimentalize things. Here I've been thinking all this time that Fred was a decent, strong, honest man; that he did not need me as my husband did. And he was a common crook; a thief; a man without principle; one who betrayed a trust; took money! (*Disgusted*) Oh, that I should ever have given him a thought! It shames me, Tom, that any man who touched my life, who claimed he loved me should not be able to go straight and honest. Oh, the insult he's given me. And then he blames me—*me*—for what he has become! (*Passionately*) Why didn't you have him arrested?

PORTER

Because it would have been your husband's duty to send him to jail.

DORA

Do you think Wallace would have hesitated in doing his duty?

PORTER

You thought you loved Fred then. You might have interfered. You might have felt responsible.

Dora

Responsible! (*Sarcastically*) That's what Fred said. (*Bitterly*) That I had wrecked his life for the sake of my husband. Oh, what a cad to say a thing like that.

Porter

I didn't want any opportunity to arise where Wallace *might* forget his oath of office.

Dora

(*With confidence*)

He wouldn't have forgotten it. He'd have gone through anything that was his duty *then*, as he would now.

Porter

Yes; I'm glad you feel *that*.

Dora

And Fred actually said Wallace was crooked.

Porter

What?

Dora

Yes. That was the last insult.

Porter

God! He was a rotter, wasn't he?

DORA

Yes. And to think I *might* have gone with him— might have been married by now—to a crook. (*Shuddering*) Oh!

(*The 'phone rings.*)

PORTER

But it's all right now, Dora.

DORA

Yes. Only make him go away. You can.

PORTER

I have already. (*She looks up in surprise*) I followed him after he left here. I *made* him sail at noon. He's gone to the land of the men who can't come back.

DORA

(*With a sigh of relief*)

Thank you, Tom. (*The 'phone rings again*) You answer it.

PORTER

Always knew you'd see you hadn't made a mistake in staying here.

DORA

(*Smiling tenderly*)

No. I didn't make any mistake.

(DORA *goes over to the piano and after a few moments sits before it, completely mistress of*

herself again. PORTER *goes to 'phone.* KENT
enters quietly and is unobserved at first.)

PORTER

Hello! Yes, this is Mr. Kent's. Cooper & Collins?
If it's *important* I'll call him.

KENT

(*Slightly embarrassed*)

Is it for me?

PORTER

(*Looking at him slowly*)

Yes; your brokers.

KENT

Tell them to hold the wire. (PORTER *does so and
puts down receiver*) Julia wouldn't come in. She and
Armor are waiting for you, Tom.

PORTER

(*Realizing* KENT *wishes to speak privately on 'phone*)
To be sure. Bye-bye, Wallace. (*Goes to* DORA,
who gives him a handshake full of gratitude) Bye-bye.
Going to take dinner with Julia to-night. (*Whimsically*) Intend to try my luck again before she goes.
Wouldn't it be splendid if she——? Well, it's something to love her even if I can't.—Bye-bye.

(PORTER *goes out.* KENT, *after glancing at*
DORA *and not desiring to arouse her suspicions,
decides to 'phone openly.*)

KENT

Hello, Collins. What do you advise? Prices have
gone down a point? You don't need more margin?
Well, don't buy in till it drops to 40. (*Significantly*)
I think it will. Good-bye.

(*He hangs up the receiver and looks at* DORA,
*who has now begun to play an improvisation.
There is a long pause. After slowly lighting a
cigarette* KENT *crosses to her. It is seen he
realizes he must make some explanation. His
manner throughout is tender and shows the
difficulty of his position.*)

I'm going to Rosemoor for a few days. Will you go
with me?

DORA

And interrupt your work? No. (*Cheerfully, as
she continues to play throughout softly*) A man should
have one place where he can get away from wives and
'phones.

KENT

Now, come, confess; you are disappointed that I'm
not in the running for Governor.

DORA

I can't seem to think of you out of public life.

KENT

Well, you see there are several big guns after the
nomination and I thought it might cause a lot of complications if I kept in as a candidate.

DORA

Yet you knew all this?

KENT

Yes, dear; but I'm getting sick of politics, with its lack of gratitude, its deals, its bickerings and fence-fixing. I've felt the need of something secure—some life position away from all the mess of campaigns and elections. (*Eyeing her*) Besides, I know how much happier you'd feel if things were certain.

DORA

(*Not quite understanding*)

But you never felt this way before. You always loved the fight. (*Smiling*) I'm afraid you'll get restless for the smell of battle, as you used to call it. You talk as though you were going to give up your whole life-work. I won't let you do that. It's just a mood, dear. You've been working too hard.

KENT

(*Puffing slowly and measuring his words carefully*)

Oh, I'm not going to put everything away.—I'll tell you a little secret. Only you must promise to keep it all to yourself till it comes out in the papers? (*She smiles in agreement*) Well—you see, there's a vacancy on the Federal Bench.

DORA

A Federal Judgeship? (*She stops playing, rises and in a puzzled manner goes to him, trying throughout to grasp its meaning*) That isn't why you've agreed to postpone this Railroad case?

KENT

(*With apparent frankness*)
Haven't I explained all that?

DORA

You've explained only that you are not going to be a candidate for Governor.

KENT

I told you they had offered it and that I refused.

DORA

The Governorship is an elective office; the people would have some say in that. Tainter and the Machine control enough Federal patronage in this boss-ridden state to offer you the Judgeship. I know that. For reasons of their own it has been offered you, as an *alternative;* and you have accepted. You have accepted, haven't you?

KENT

Well, what if I have? Do you suppose, Dora, that I'd have been foolish enough to have told you this at all, if I had meant to deceive you?

DORA

You've seen my suspicions. You realized that you couldn't always keep this from me. Perhaps you thought the best way to blind me was to tell me the truth.

KENT

(*Turning away*)

Have we got to go over this again?

DORA

I must understand this; I must think what this means.

KENT

Aren't you women happier when you don't think?

DORA

Please don't treat me as a child. If all this hadn't happened just when it did I'd have taken your mere word. But I can't. I can't *now*.

KENT

Dora!

DORA

Wallace; since luncheon yesterday I *have* been tortured in spite of myself. You could have seen me there by the window when you four passed through this room. (*He is startled*) I couldn't help hearing. Gilmore said it could be made to 'appear' all right.

You've done so to Armor; but you must tell me the truth.

KENT

It hasn't been pleasant for me to deceive Armor. I beg of you not to go any further.

DORA

(*Slowly*)

So they accomplished their object in coming?

KENT

Since you insist on knowing—yes.

DORA

You've agreed to delay prosecuting the C. N. Y. case?

KENT

Don't forget how financial and political interests are allied.

DORA

(*Admitting it to herself for the first time*)

And in return they will see that you get a Federal Judgeship!

KENT

Now, don't blame me. You don't know what's back of this.

DORA

(*With a ray of hope*)

I'm only trying to see if it's honest, that's all?

KENT

There's nothing illegal——

DORA

I'm not talking of law. I'm talking of what's right.
You've agreed to delay the course of justice for your
own political advancement. Isn't that what it practically means?

KENT

I'm seeing this through my need; so don't ask me
anything further. I've done what I thought expedient
and best for you.

DORA

(*Surprised*)

You've done this for me?

KENT

I said you were part of my reason for agreeing.
(*Testily*) Good Heavens, Dora; many wives would be
proud to be in your position.

DORA

I have been proud of your success up to now. Success! (*Recalls* JULIA'S *words*) But success is not
the test.

KENT

It's the American standard.

DORA

I could never forget how you had obtained the appointment. (*He moves away as though dismissing it. She hesitates a moment and then goes to him tenderly*) Wallace; several times things like this have come up in the past and we've always talked them over together. Remember that Insurance case last Fall? You said I helped you then. I know men in politics and public office must consider many factors, and they can't help thinking, in spite of themselves, of the political effect. Let's talk this over, too; if it's a case like that.

KENT

But I've already agreed to this.

DORA

You have? (WALLACE *nods*) If you've done this through some mistaken desire to satisfy me, there's still time to——

KENT

I can't. (*In spite of himself*) There are *other* reasons.

DORA

Reasons that *compel* you to do it?

KENT

Does a man do these things of choice?

DORA

If it's the easiest way, some do; but you never took
that cut. (*As the suspicion slowly grows*) Do they
know something about you?

KENT

Yes.

DORA

Something dishonest that you—you've done? And
for their silence——?

KENT

No. I've done nothing dishonest—yet.

DORA

(*She gives a quick gasp of joy which slowly turns into
another suspicion*)
This telephone just now. Your brokers! Stocks!

KENT

(*Quickly*)
For God's sake, Dora, don't dig too deep, I tell you.

DORA

(*Point blank*)
Has it to do with money?

KENT

Yes.

DORA

(*Shrinking away*)

You, *too!*

KENT

(*Brutally*)

Yes: I need money. Now you've got it.

DORA

(*Gasping at him absolutely stunned*)

You're taking their *money?*

KENT

No; I'm not as crude as that. I've sold stocks I haven't got, on margin. Nothing illegal in that. Just the habit of a nation.

DORA

(*After a pause, as though trying to grasp it*)

Go on! I don't understand.

KENT

I'm caught in the market. Gilmore and Biddle and their friends control a pool of the stock; they will force prices down so I can buy in and get out and make what I need. (*Bitterly*) In return for their consideration, I merely delay the C. N. Y. trial.

DORA

(*Almost inaudibly as she recalls* SAFFORD'S *accusation*)
Then he was right!

KENT

(*Desperately*)
You don't know what it is to need money, do you?

DORA

(*Vaguely for some moments*)
No.   You've always given me everything; I have a
little income of my own, too——

KENT

Your income pays for your flowers and your music;
but what of your carriages, your amusements?

DORA

(*Dumbly*)
But your salary?

KENT

Paid for your dresses and pretty things.

DORA

(*Confused*)
But I didn't know; I didn't know.

KENT

Why should you? You never could understand money matters.

DORA

(*Helplessly*)

I always thought we had enough. You never said anything about my accounts. I've let you handle everything.

KENT

(*Half tenderly*)

I haven't been particularly anxious for you to know the facts. (*She looks at him*) No matter why. Perhaps because you took such joy in pretty things.

DORA

(*Quietly*)

You feel I'm partly to blame for your financial condition. Yes; you do. Well, fortunately, it's not too late; we'll change all that.

KENT

(*Shrugging his shoulders*)

Change a habit in a moment?

DORA

I can try. I'll do without my ' pretty things,' as you call them. There, there, Wallace. We can live on what we have, can't we?

KENT

And what of the bills?

DORA

(*Good-naturedly*)

They can wait.

KENT

(*Laughs*)

I've paid nothing for months. Many of them have threatened suit. It's a marvel the yellow newspapers——

DORA

Can't we save?

KENT

Who ever lives in this city and saves?

DORA

(*Cheerfully*)

We will.

KENT

Yes; after I get on my feet.

DORA

Through your deal with these men?

KENT

Yes. Now do you understand?

Dora

(*With calm determination*)

I'm willing to bear my part in whatever sacrifices we must make; but we'll make them together. Telephone Mr. Gilmore, or Mr. Tainter, that you won't do this.

Kent

Do you know what'll happen? Gilmore will *ruin* me. Ruin! We'd have to move from this house; it's mortgaged to the limit; we'd have to get rid of every piece of furniture to feed our creditors; we'd land on the streets. Every dollar I could scrape together I've put up for margin on stocks these men control. I've gone deeper and deeper; every month selling more; putting up more margin; thinking prices would drop and I could recover everything. I can't get out and they'll call on me to deliver the stuff I haven't got; and if I don't delay this Railroad case, Gilmore will push the prices up, my margins will be wiped out clean, and we'll be without a cent.

Dora

(*Calmly*)

Ruin? Move from *here?* (*Looks about room affectionately*) Well, Wallace, I'm ready even for that.

Kent

But I'm not.

DORA

I can share your poverty but not——

KENT

Come, come; look the facts in the face.

DORA

You'll not do this.

KENT

I must.

DORA

(*With calm strength*)

You will do as I say.

KENT

Nothing can make me.

DORA

I can make you. (*He looks at her in astonishment*)
Wallace, I beg of you don't do this. I beg of you. If
you only knew how I'm clinging to your honesty, what
it means to me!

KENT

There's no use in further words. (*Emphatically*)
It's done and agreed to.

DORA

(*Drawing back*)

You mean that?

KENT

Absolutely.

DORA

What about your oath of office?

KENT

Bah! Who'll know?

DORA

I'll know.

KENT

(*Cynically*)

Then I think I can trust you to keep the family secret.

DORA

Do you actually mean you're deliberately going to ruin your whole record like this?

KENT

There's many a man whose record is good because he hasn't been found out. This is nobody's concern.

DORA

Your honesty is my concern; your work is my concern; your career is my concern: not just because I'm your wife; but because I've made an equal contribution; because I have rights here. I tell you, this goes deeper than you know. I'd rather lose your love—yes —I'd rather destroy whatever happiness you have found in me, than let you make this *crooked* deal. Now you see how dead in earnest I am.

KENT

Well, I've made my choice. After all, it's *my* career.

DORA

You don't think I've been *any* part of it?

KENT

Oh, yes; in a way, but——

DORA

(*Murmuring his words, incredulously*)

In a way, but——

KENT

Well, I guess I've got a right to do what I want with my own life.

DORA

That wasn't the way I looked at it when I had a choice to make. I thought of *you* and how my actions might affect your life. You've got to think of *me* in what you do with your life!

KENT

(*Looking at her intently*)

What do you mean?

DORA

For the last time, will you telephone Gilmore?

KENT

(*Taking her by the arms imperatively*)

What choice did you ever have to make that affected my career?

DORA

You're going through with this deal?

KENT

Yes!

DORA

Then I'll answer your question.—Do you remember Fred Safford?

KENT

What of him?

DORA

During your first campaign for the District Attorneyship, he and I saw a great deal of each other.

KENT

Well?

DORA

He wanted me to go away with him. (KENT *gazes at her*) I very nearly went.

KENT

(*Hardly believing her words*)
You nearly went with him!

DORA

Yes.

KENT

And you stayed——?

DORA

(*In a clear, direct manner*)
For the reason I've just told you. You were making your first real fight. I knew how close it was. All your opponents were trying to get something on you—anything that could blur the clean-cut moral issues you were standing for. I felt a scandal could never have been explained before election; you would have been blamed somehow. I did not want you to know of Fred at the time. It would have distracted you, weakened your strength for the fight. I did not wish to postpone a decision for some future settlement. I feared I could not hide it from you much longer, so I sent him away. I gave him up. I stayed with you. I thought you needed me more; thought you needed the help I could bring you through standing by your side.

That was the choice *I* made for your career: that's
why I have a right to ask that you keep it clean.

> (*He has stood gazing at her, though at first
> unable to grasp its relation to the deal with the
> men. Then he walks back and forth several
> times in silence as though trying to make up his
> mind. She stands watching him, firm and de-
> termined yet without any defiance. Finally he
> gives a sharp, ironic laugh, as though some hid-
> den thought were touched.*)

Please don't laugh.

KENT

If only you knew how amusing it all is!

DORA

Amusing?

KENT

Yes; damned amusing.

> (*He starts for the 'phone.*)

DORA

Yes, the ending *is* amusing.   (*Starting to explain*)
I've seen Fred again.   He came back and——

KENT

Hello?   Give me Garden 77.   Yes.

Dora

I want to tell you everything, Wallace. I didn't before, because——

Kent

(*Ignoring her*)

Hello; connect me with Mr. Gilmore. Yes, Wallace Kent. Thank you. (*She waits in suspense*) Hello, Gilmore: I have been thinking over that little matter and I have decided I won't do it. (Dora *gives a cry of joy*) No; under no considerations. Personal reasons. Yes. (*Significantly*) I quite appreciate what it means. Good-bye.

(*He puts back receiver.*)

Dora

(*Deeply moved*)

Thank you—thank you.

Kent

(*Coldly*)

What's Armor's number?

Dora

I never can remember figures. (*As he glances through telephone book*) Thank you. It's all clean and above board now. We'll get along somehow. It may not be as hard as you suppose. We'll move to a cheaper place. I'll never forget this, never, never.

KENT

(*At the 'phone*)

Give me Morris 176.

DORA

I'm sure there'll be something I can do. (*Trying to smile*) I never was very handy with my fingers, but, if necessary, I'll do *anything* that will help.

KENT

(*At 'phone*)

Hello! Is that you, Armor? Just get in? Well, I've come to the conclusion you're right about that C. N. Y. business and I'll let you take it into court yourself next Monday.—I thought you'd be pleased. Can you open the case without me? I may have to be out of town for a few days, so I'll leave everything in your hands. Yes, of course you can tell Julia. Good-bye. Don't thank *me*.

(*He hangs up receiver.*)

DORA

(*She goes to put her arms around him with a flood of affection*)

What can I say?

KENT

(*Pushing her gently away*)

I intend to send to the Governor to-night my resignation as District Attorney.

DORA

(*Slowly*)

Your resignation?

KENT

Yes.

DORA

Why?

KENT

Because I can accept nothing at the price you paid nor keep what I've gained by it. (*She is completely stunned and he continues with increasing bitterness*) Was that your idea of my character, my strength? Did you think I could not have stood *alone?*

DORA

I only thought you needed me.

KENT

I did not need your pity.

DORA

You did not know what it was I gave you; the effect was the same.

KENT

At the time, yes.

DORA

I gave it all willingly.

KENT

You expect me to take it proudly because you sacrificed yourself and the man you loved for fear I might go to pieces? You thought I couldn't rise above talk? Proud of *that?* It's an insult.

DORA

(*Completely halted by his unexpected reaction*)
Insult?

KENT

Yes; it was an insult: you might have given me the chance to offer you happiness with your poor weak fool. (*She starts to explain*) Do you believe I'd have dragged you away from him or punished you because *I* couldn't keep your love? Do you think I couldn't have been decent to you both?

DORA

You would have treated me decently, I know. But that wouldn't have altered the *other* facts. I did what I thought was honorable by you.

KENT

(*Sneering*)

Honorable? Honorable? You women are funny! You're shocked at me because I accepted Gilmore's offer; yet with your feminine logic you can see nothing despicable in living a lie in my house. Honorable?

DORA

(*Confused*)

No! No! I lived no lie. If you'll let me explain.
I suffered for it at first, but——

KENT

That was sufficient excuse I suppose for the deceit?
Only suffer for an action, you women think, and it becomes beautiful! Suffer! You love it; you take pleasure
in it; your spirit of martyrdom is your greatest luxury.
Well, you acted well; played your part splendidly;
for I never suspected, even when he was around.

DORA

(*Forcefully*)

Then give me credit for that. There would have
been no sacrifice had I brought you only tears. What
if I did hide all that was hard *then?* You blame me
for the lie; give me credit for my consideration and
sincerity.

KENT

Sincerity? And you lived with me all this time as
my wife and I never knew!

DORA

What else could I do if I stayed with you?

KENT

Wanton!

DORA

(*Flaming up*)

Don't you dare——

KENT

I understand now. You took my name, my roof, my protection, and gave yourself in return. (*She gives a sharp cry*) Wanton! You took lips that meant his; embraces that made other memories live. And his name! How was it you never gasped his name?

DORA

I never stole one hour with him. I played straight that way.

KENT

How do I know, how can I *ever* know?

DORA

I'm giving you my word!

KENT

(*With great scorn*)

Your word! When you lived this lie and have given everything the same! (*She turns to deny but can scarcely speak at his attitude*) How can I believe anything in the present or past just because you've given your word?

(*She stands stunned at his words as he begins to laugh ironically throughout.*)

DORA

If that's the way you feel, you can believe anything you wish!

KENT

Haven't you gone on cheating him, cheating yourself, and cheating me?

DORA

You?

KENT

Yes, *me!* And I thought all the while *I* was the one you loved. I fooled myself that I was everything to you. And I wasn't, was I? I wasn't?

DORA

I tell you nothing more till you come to your senses.

KENT

I'm in my right senses. I see it all. *You* don't have to explain. But I do. I want you to know I, also, did everything I could to fool and deceive you.

DORA

(*Starting up*)

To fool *me?*

KENT

Yes. I heaped pretty things upon you, gave you everything you wished; I've ruined myself—everything.

Now you see. Now you see why this is too monstrously funny. Because I thought you loved me and that kept *me* silent.

DORA

Silent? (*Going to him*) What are you talking about?

KENT

Don't you see? You love somebody else. I am nothing to you now. I can pass out of your life, it's over.

DORA

(*Trying to break in*)

Answer me. What have *you* been silent about?

KENT

Now that it's all over between us, I can tell you. Don't think I want your pity. I don't need it now that we know we do not love each other.

DORA

(*Starting back*)

You don't love me?

KENT

What difference does *my* love make to you now?

DORA

But——

KENT

Let's stop. It's over. Done with. Thrown in the rubbish heap.

DORA

Let's have all the truth.

KENT

It's too late, I tell you; too late for me.

DORA

(*Trying to grasp the situation*)
You don't love me.

KENT

I never guessed about you. You never guessed about me. What a game we were playing. And you could have seen it happen right *here,* before your eyes.

DORA

(*Grasping it*)
She lied to me! You love her! Julia!

KENT

Isn't it funny that you should love somebody else and that I should love somebody else and that we should go on living together, lying to each other? Isn't it too monstrously comical?

DORA

(*Passionately*)

Yes, that you could live with me when your love had ceased; give everything just the same, because you were a man. You could fool and trick me and yet blame me. That's why you were so bitter; I wounded your pride and not your love!

KENT

I know, I know, you're right. I won't sneak out of it the injured party. I was to blame, I was to blame, I was cruel—all. I lied; I lied. We both lied. And look what has happened.

DORA

(*Quickly*)

All that's happened is that I'm in the way. That can be changed. Go to her.

KENT

(*Halting*)

Why to *her*, pray?

DORA

(*Controlling herself*)

She loves you.

KENT

Me? Loves me? (*Laughing as before*) Loves me? When I've never said a word, never dared look her in the eyes because I didn't want to mess things up and make you unhappy? Loves me? No, no.

DORA

(*With cold intensity*)

Go to her. She loves you. She told me.

KENT

That's absurd. Why should she tell you? It isn't true. No. No. It can't be true.

DORA

Go to her; she loves you.

KENT

(*Dismissing it*)

I've had enough of love and lies. There's nothing more to say. (*Goes to the door*) I'll leave the house to-night and go to Rosemoor; later you and I can arrange matters quietly.

DORA

(*With a sharp cry*)

And what's to become of me?

KENT

(*Bitterly*)

Now *you* can go to the man you love!
(*He goes out.   She stands stunned and silent.*)

CURTAIN

THE THIRD ACT

THE THIRD ACT

The study in JULIA DEERING'S *apartment. The same evening: later.*

The room, which is shallow and intimate, is soft in tone. The fireplace at the left contains a blazing log which casts its wavering light upon a deep leather couch stretched cata-cornered before it. Several long cathedral candles, in esthetic holders, are also lighted, and one notices a work-table near the center, upon which are a writer's usual assortment of disordered letters and manuscripts. There are several chairs, of varying designs, about this. Above it hangs a soft shaded light-cluster which, when the curtain lifts, is turned out. Several old engravings are seen, otherwise the walls seem to melt away in the shadows. The floor is covered with a thick Oriental rug. The room, somehow, suggests JULIA—*with its faintly insinuating appeal to sensation.*

The general entrance is in the right upper corner of the irregularly cut room. This door opens out upon the hallway which leads to the rest of the apartment. A window, now curtained, with some low book-cases on either side, is in the back. The electric switch is by the fireplace.

There is no one visible when the curtain rises. Some moments later JULIA *opens the door and comes in, followed by* PORTER, *who is eyeing her furtively.*

She wears a loose informal gown; he is in dinner-coat.
She goes towards the fire and sits upon the couch.

JULIA

The cigarettes are there, Tom.

PORTER

Have one?

JULIA
(Taking it)
Try one of mine. They're a new brand, Russian.
Safonoff sent them to me.

PORTER
(As he lights her cigarette)
No; I'll stick by my own.

JULIA

(After a pause, as he gazes at her blowing rings)
I love to watch the smoke.

PORTER

I love to watch you watch it.
(A MAID *enters with coffee cups on tray which*
she places near JULIA. *She fills them with*
steaming coffee; hands one to JULIA *and offers*
the other to PORTER, *who takes it. She then*
goes to switch on the light.)

JULIA

Don't turn up the lights yet. (MAID *goes out.*)
I'm so fond of shadows. Aren't you, Tom?

PORTER

Depends on whom I happen to be with.

JULIA

Oh, I forgot your sugar.

PORTER

(*Refusing it*)
Doctor's orders; getting old, Julia.

JULIA

You'll always be the same to me.

PORTER

(*Bantering throughout*)
Sounds discouraging already.

JULIA

Discouraging? You didn't intend to ask me to
marry you *again?*

PORTER

You haven't married me once yet.

JULIA

I'm a better friend.

PORTER

I like adventure.

JULIA

I thought you were seeking peace and quiet.

PORTER

No; I'm seeking a wife. They're not necessarily synonymous.

JULIA

But peace and quiet only can come with love, *n'est-ce pas?*

PORTER

Nonsense. There's nothing reasoning or reasonable about love. It drags people together who'd be much better apart. It frequently pulls one away from two and makes sixes or sevens. It steals like a sneak thief where it shouldn't go and dodges the vacuums where it would be welcome. Love sometimes raises a family, Julia—(*Mock confidentially*)—but more often it raises the devil. And when our law-makers are trying to pin it down, it only laughs at them. Why don't these anti-divorcers and preachers and professional moralists stop chiding the poor creatures in love and try to devise some apparatus to steer the pesky thing right? I'll patent it and give it to humanity without royalty.

JULIA

(*Amused*)

Tom, I know just where I can use that idea in my new novel.

PORTER

I forbid it unless you'll marry me.

JULIA

(*She shakes her head*)

Take another cigarette instead.

PORTER

Hardly a substitute.—I'll stop making love if you won't go abroad. You know, I don't like the idea of getting plastery picture postal cards of Corfu in the moonlight.

JULIA

(*Musing*)

You want to marry me. I wonder what would happen if *I* had what I sought most?

PORTER

(*Dryly*)

You spend too much time anticipating your emotions. When they come, you have already lived through them. The experience itself never can equal such anticipation.

JULIA

The penalty of all writers.

PORTER

Why, you've got everything now: money, beauty, temperament, reputation; everything you should have.

JULIA

But a husband?

PORTER

I offer to supply the deficiency.

JULIA

I'd make you miserable. Tom, why didn't you fall in love with some sweet young woman with pretty pink ribbons and pussy-cat ways?

PORTER

I did. But she refused me; fortunately. (*Whimsically exaggerating*) Come to think of it, I guess I've gone through the entire repertoire. Every time an adorable woman broke my heart I read the history of some foreign country to restore me to my proper place in the universe. When we suffer we're so self-centered. I've only got Persia left. (*Sighing*) Please save me from Persia. I hate the Shahs with their sneezable names.

JULIA

(*Smiling*)

You'd forget me, as you have the others.

PORTER

This is my finish—after Persia. (*With his real feeling escaping for the first time*) Why, dear Julia; don't you suppose I know how foolish it is of me asking you? You were made for the men who could shoot you to the stars and whirl you till you were dizzy in their dust, and all that literary sort of stuff. But you'll not be happy that way. I'm not much on star dust. Then I'm not young any more. Oh, I acknowledge it officially. I'm only one of the wanderers on the streets below with a hand waiting to help a woman just a little now and then. (*Taking her hand*) I know it's foolish, but I'd like to see some quiet come into that restless soul of yours; I'd like to make you— *quietly* happy. That's all.

JULIA

Quietly happy! (*With deep feeling*) Don't go out of my life; I need you 'just around the corner' as you said to Dora; for I'm a miserable woman at times, struggling with impulses which drive women like me to—. But you steady me. You're a sort of habit. I need you. I'd have tried to take much I had no right to if you hadn't been here. (*Impetuously as she thinks of* WALLACE) I would now if—. I tell you, there's a courage that accepts but a greater courage that dares.

PORTER

(*Not understanding*)

Julia!

JULIA

(*Dismissing it*)

Ah, *je suis égarée!*

PORTER

Don't know what it is, but you've got it.

JULIA

(*Laughing again as her mood changes*)

Forgive me.   Don't say anything more of love; but be just around the corner.

PORTER

(*Resigned*)

You can do the Rock of Ages act all over me.   Grab hold any time; I'll let you cling and won't call for help.

JULIA

Tom, I could kiss you.

PORTER

But something always happens to prevent.   (MAID *knocks and enters.*)   Didn't I tell you?

MAID

I beg pardon.

JULIA

What is it?

MAID

I forgot to say Mrs. Kent telephoned ten minutes
ago that she was on her way over to see you.

JULIA

(*Surprised*)

Mrs. Kent?

MAID

Yes, ma'am.

JULIA

Let her come right in here.
(MAID *goes out.* JULIA, *somewhat puzzled
by this announcement, goes slowly to the lights
and switches them on.* PORTER *gazes at her a
few seconds, gives a little sigh as though realizing the uselessness of further words. Then he
looks at his watch.*)

PORTER

Goodness, I must trot along. Promised to drop in
on Armor. I've got a warm place in my heart for
that brother of yours. I'll leave you and Dora here to
pow-wow.

JULIA

I wonder why Dora's coming to see me?

PORTER

Perhaps Wallace had to go to his office. He's got that very important case on.

JULIA

(*As she abstractedly puts out the candles*)
But don't you remember? He said he was going off this evening by himself to Rosemoor.

PORTER

Oh, yes; that's so. Think I'll get a bungalow like that when you've gone.

JULIA

Rosemoor! It's such a pretty name.

PORTER

Wallace has a lot of sentiment down deep which law books haven't killed. If you'd see that view over the valley and not a soul to share it with him.

JULIA

(*Wistfully*)
I've always thought I'd like to see it before I went away.

PORTER

But he plays the primitive there and keeps house himself. It takes a touch of poetry these days to get

away from people and 'phones.—Well, I must be going.
Tell Dora I couldn't wait.

JULIA

Tom, I've been waiting for you to tell me what
happened between Fred and Dora.

PORTER

Dora can tell that better. Perhaps that's why she's
coming over.

JULIA

Fred's gone away?

PORTER

Yes; he sailed at noon.

JULIA

(*Puzzled*)

But how did she *make* him go?

PORTER

(*Smiling*)

Some day, I'll let you know—if she doesn't.
    (DORA *enters. She is simply dressed and wears
    a scarf over her head. She is very calm and
    deliberate throughout with a certain firm
    strength. They greet, and* PORTER *takes off
    her cloak, throwing it on chair.*)

JULIA

Come near the fire, Dora; the nights are still chilly. (JULIA *crosses to fire with* DORA) I'll send for some hot coffee.

DORA

No; thanks.

PORTER

Sorry I was just running off.

DORA

Must you?

JULIA

Tom's going to see Armor.

DORA

Then take my taxi, Tom. But send it right back. I'll only be here a few moments.

(JULIA *looks surprised.*)

PORTER

Thanks. Any messages for Armor?

DORA

Tell him I'm glad he's going to conduct the C. N. Y. case.

PORTER

(*Deeply pleased*)

I knew Wallace would do what was right by him.

DORA

Yes; he does what he sees is right, too.

PORTER

(*Quietly to* DORA *as* JULIA *has crossed to desk for some letters*)

Was worried this afternoon. Good-bye, little girl.

DORA

You've told Julia about Fred?

PORTER

Only that he's gone away.

DORA

I want you to come around in the morning. I need some advice about a trip I'm going to take.

PORTER

(*Surprised*)

Certainly.

JULIA

(*Handing him some letters*)

Tom, will you mail these? Please don't forget them. One is about my passport.

PORTER

(*Taking them*)

The instrument of my own destruction, eh? (*Looking at it*) Sort of Greek irony. But don't worry, I'll mail it. Bye-bye. Rock of Ages any time you're willing. See you to-morrow, Dora. Bye-bye.

(*He goes out. JULIA follows him off a second. They are heard talking. DORA is left alone. She relaxes a moment as though feeling she has not the strength to go through what she has apparently determined upon. Her eyes fall upon KENT'S photograph, which is with some others on mantel. She takes it down and smiles at it enigmatically, replacing it as JULIA returns. She assumes a steely exterior as JULIA, obviously sensing a deep reason for DORA'S coming, closes the door and comes down. There is a pause.*)

DORA

Wallace has not been here?

JULIA

(*Surprised*)

Why, no.

DORA

He wrote some letters but went out before I did. I thought——

JULIA

Wallace went to Rosemoor, didn't he?

DORA

Oh, yes; perhaps.

JULIA

How did you think he'd be here?

DORA

Because I told him to go to you.

JULIA

You told him to see me? What about?

DORA

Julia, he and I have gone on the rocks at last.

JULIA

I don't understand.

DORA

It's very simple. It's all over between us.

JULIA

(*Hardly grasping the significance*)
What do you mean?

DORA

He doesn't love me.

JULIA

What are you saying?

DORA

He has ceased to love me.

JULIA

(*With mingled emotions*)
Then—then you *are* going to Fred?

DORA

(*With a bitter laugh*)
Going to Fred? That's over, too.

JULIA

(*Eyeing* DORA)
But why did you send Wallace here?

DORA

Because I am going to leave him. (JULIA *gazes incredulously*) You said you'd like to have had a chance for happiness. I give you more than a chance. When he and I came to talk it all over (*With difficulty*) I found it—it was *you* he cared for.

JULIA

Me?

DORA

Yes.

JULIA

Wallace cares for me?

DORA

Yes; and he knows you love him.

JULIA

You told him that?

DORA

(*Firmly*)

Yes: you both must not miss your happiness.

JULIA

It isn't so; it can't be so.

DORA

Would I lie to you now after our talk yesterday?

JULIA

Wallace loves me! He loves me—*me!*
   (JULIA *sinks down in the chair, half dazed.*
   DORA *stands watching her without emotion.*
   JULIA *slowly recovers; there is a long silence*

then she gradually looks at DORA *with a new thought.)*
And you? What are you going to do?

DORA

I told you. I'm going to leave Wallace. (*Bitterly*)
He said I should go to the man I love.

JULIA

He knows about Fred?

DORA

Yes. But he thinks I love Fred and that I am going
to him. Wallace must always believe that.

JULIA

But that's a lie.

DORA

Isn't it better to lie if it will bring you happiness?

JULIA

You believe the truth might separate him and me?
You think if he *should* know you do not love Fred——

DORA

I don't wish him to have any thought of me. (*Bitterly*) Even men pity sometimes.

JULIA

(*Incredulously*)

And you can ask me to keep a secret like that?

DORA

Most women keep secrets from the men they love.

JULIA

(*Determined*)

No; he must know the facts.

DORA

But *his* happiness lies in your silence about Fred and me.

JULIA

(*Pointedly*)

And what of *my* happiness? You've put a fear in it. You've settled your own lives but I'm the factor you don't seem to have considered. (*Resolutely*) No; he must understand about you first, or I'd always be asking myself afterwards what would Wallace have done if he'd known the truth? Would he have left Dora *alone?*—No, no, I can't.

DORA

(*Coldly*)

You must not think of me.

JULIA

But I do, Dora. I could never forget you. I'd always see you alone.

DORA

I've always been helpless Dora to you, haven't I? Just because I wasn't practical, as you called it. But I did what I thought was the greatest thing a woman could for her husband; yet in his wounded pride he thought I should have gone to Fred. Oh, not from any generosity on his part; but because I had stood between you and him. (JULIA *surprised*) He didn't realize it himself, perhaps; but *I* won't be in the way any longer. Never—never could I live with him after what he said to me. I'm leaving him for good. I would even if you were not concerned. That's why I've come to ask you to be silent about Fred and me.

JULIA

The lie of silence!

DORA

Julia. Be fair to him. I gave him his chance by telling him you love him. You mustn't rob him of it. You love him, don't you? (JULIA *bows her head*) Then make him happy!

JULIA

(*Rising quickly*)

How did *this* all so suddenly come about? (*Going to her*) Dora, *was* it because I told you what he meant to me?

DORA

(*Confused a second at the abruptness*)

No.

JULIA

Nothing *he* did or said about me?

DORA

No; nothing he said about you.

JULIA

It wasn't I who came between you?

DORA

(*Evasively*)

No; it simply happened. We were talking. How are things ever discovered? Time found us out. Time's a rummager, isn't it? See how it found out you two loved each other.

JULIA

(*Half to herself as she sits down still unable to grasp the fact*)

That we two love each other!

DORA

(*Earnestly*)

Before I go; before you see him; say you will be silent about Fred. (JULIA *hesitates*) Think, Julia, of Wallace. Don't you see it's best he should believe me happy. Make it easier for him and I'll simply step aside. Come, Julia, say you will. It's not a falsehood I ask; it's only silence.

JULIA

Silence can be so cowardly. (*Hesitates*) Yet—I— I——

DORA

But you two love each other. It's *I* now who asks love to take its right—since I made such a mess of mine. (JULIA *bows her head.* DORA *looks at her and sees she has practically consented.*) I wish him to be happy more than anything else in the world.

JULIA

(*Quickly*)

Dora! *You* love him!

DORA

No, no, no! He killed everything in me. I'll prove it when the time comes.

JULIA

(*Stands confused*)

You love him!

DORA

No.

(*A knock is heard on the door.*)

JULIA

What is it?

(MAID *opens the door.*)

MAID

Mr. Kent is here.

(*There is a tense moment.* JULIA *looks inquiringly at* DORA, *who quickly decides what to do.*)

DORA

(*Calmly*)

Let him come in, Julia.

JULIA

(*Confused*)

But——

DORA

(*Firmly*)

We three must understand one another.

JULIA

(*Trying to gain composure*)

Ask Mr. Kent to come in.   Put a log there.

(MAID *goes over to fire and puts on another log which blazes cheerfully.   They half watch her during the ominous silence.*)

Tell Mr. Kent that Mrs. Kent is here with me.   I

sha'n't need you any more to-night. (MAID *goes out, leaving the door open*) It's best Wallace knows you are here.

DORA

He will not go away. And he will want you to know I do not love him. (*She stands by fire warming her hands*) The fire is good.

JULIA

I'm burning. (*Turning away; half to herself*) What shall I do? (*After a pause*) And this is Dora.

DORA

(*Simply*)

One changes.

(*There is a further silence till* KENT *enters slowly as though the fact that* DORA *is there has made him hesitate. He closes the door and stands looking at the two women. He cannot conceal entirely the bitterness of the previous scene with his wife.*)

Again, it's a bit ironical, isn't it, Wallace? (*He is silent*) But there need be no embarrassment on my account.

KENT

I came to say good-bye to Julia.

DORA

I knew you would come.

KENT

And your reason for being here?

DORA

To tell her what she means to you.

KENT

(*Emphatically*)

I did not come to talk of that.

DORA

When I told you she loved you, you said it wasn't true. Ask her now.

KENT

Believe me, Julia, I did not come to ask any questions; as you shall see before I go.

DORA

Ask her. I want everything clearly understood. (KENT *in silence, looks towards* JULIA, *who sinks into the chair, burying her face in her hands*) You see, Wallace.

KENT

Well, Dora, is that all?

DORA

No. I'm thinking we'd best talk the matter over quietly.

KENT

Here?

DORA

Why not? It would have to be some time and now it will be finished sooner. There must be no skeins to unravel later among us there; we must understand one another now. Won't you sit down, Wallace?

> (KENT *hesitates, but seeing the cold determination in* DORA'S *manner, he goes slowly to the other side of the table. After glancing at* JULIA, *who is in the deep chair gazing tensely before her, he draws back the chair and sits upon it. After this is done,* DORA *goes to the other chair back of table, between them. The light from the lamp falls upon the three.*)

Wallace, Julia knows that you and I have gone on the rocks.

KENT

(*Referring to the political deal*)

Is that *all* you've told her?

DORA

Yes.

KENT

(*Significantly*)

Nothing else, Julia?

DORA

(*Quickly*)

You doubt my word?

JULIA

(*Looking up suspiciously*)

What else was there I should know?

DORA

(*Clearly*)

Nothing.

KENT

Then you had no other reason for coming?

DORA

(*Firmly*)

Yes: I came to tell Julia that I was going to the man I love, so that you and she should face the future without thought of me—together.

KENT

(*Sarcastically*)

I could have told her that, if ever the time should come.

DORA

It was right *I* should do that much for her, since I am going to be happy, too.

KENT

Happy? You're sure of that, eh?

DORA

Would your vanity desire me to suffer in losing you? You've shown me once today that pride is as deep and cruel as love.

KENT

I was harsh, perhaps; but——

DORA

Don't have any regret now. I have none, at leaving you. (*He winces*) But I desire Julia to understand how far you and I are apart.

KENT

(*Bitterly*)

Is that all you have to say?

DORA

(*Concealing from them her suffering*)

No. I have a further word to add to my confession. It wasn't really the thought of you and your career that made me stay with you, as I said. I stayed because I hadn't the courage to go through all that was necessary. I stayed, like so many other wives, because it was easier.

KENT
(*Disgusted*)
That destroys everything between us.

DORA
I meant it to.
(*She rises and turns away.*)

KENT
(*Coldly*)
There will be essential affairs to talk over.

DORA
When you come back from Rosemoor will be time enough. Now I'm through here.

KENT
(*Coldly*)
What do you intend to do?

DORA
I shall go West to my cousin. I'll stay the requisite time for the divorce. Perhaps Tom will advise me. We'll both go through the usual mockery: desertion and all that. Then life will begin again.

KENT

(*Cut, but puzzled by her manner*)

After all these years, you can say only that?
(JULIA *looks up slowly and inquiringly at him
as though wondering whether he has feeling for*
DORA. *Over* DORA'S *face there is a momentary
glance of tenderness which, under* JULIA'S *in-
quiring look, assumes coldness as before.*)

DORA

Yes, Wallace. I'm glad it's over. That's all there
is left. Good-bye.
(*She picks up her long scarf, puts it about her.*)

KENT

(*Abruptly*)

And Gilmore? You didn't tell Julia about——?

DORA

(*Quickly*)

No, Wallace. Let that be between us.

KENT

(*Scornfully*)

More lies!

JULIA

(*Starting up*)

Lies?

KENT

Yes. Rotten lies.

DORA

(*Nervously*)

Wallace!

KENT

I said I didn't come here to talk of love. I came for only one purpose: to tell Julia about Gilmore and Tainter, and what had happened between us.

DORA

Why say anything?

JULIA

(*Quickly, rising*)

Then there *was* something that brought about the break between you?

DORA

I told you everything, Julia.

JULIA

You told me nothing.

DORA

But it hadn't anything to do with *you.*

KENT

No. It was something wrong with *me.* I've written my resignation, Julia. My career is done, finished, thrown aside.

JULIA

(*Quickly*)

You feared some scandal would result in coming to me as Dora once feared it in going to——?

DORA

(*Confused at new turn of situation*)

No! No! Nothing like that.

JULIA

It *was* something to do with me. I came between you.

KENT

(*Sarcastically*)

I gave it all up for Dora's justification.

JULIA

(*Recalling*)

Justification!

KENT

Tell her, Dora, I faced an alternative; to stop meant financial ruin.

JULIA

And you stopped?

KENT

Yes; we are ruined, on the streets without a penny.

JULIA

(*Astonished*)

Then Dora has nothing?

KENT

(*Bitterly*)

You forget she has the other man!

JULIA

(*Starting to reveal the truth*)

But——

DORA

(*Stopping her*)

Hush! Your happiness should be your first thought!

JULIA

(*Hesitating*)

Oh!

KENT

You said, Dora, we were to talk it over calmly in order that Julia and I should start straight. I intend to see whether you and I, Julia, can ever start at all.

DORA

(*Desperately trying to stop him*)

Wallace!

JULIA

Whether——?

KENT

(*Bitterly to* DORA)

You came here tonight to arrange matters. Perhaps you didn't trust me. So tell her about Gilmore and all the rest.

DORA

Wallace, will you be silent about that? That's ours —*ours*. I have the right to ask some silence of our life together.

KENT

But first tell her I'm a crook; a bribe-taker; anything you choose to call it.

JULIA

Wallace!

DORA

(*Noting* JULIA'S *reaction and defending him*)
That isn't so, Julia.

KENT

(*Sarcastically*)

Tell her it's intention that makes crime. Tell her, as I was going to, that you discovered I wasn't quite the ideal man you thought me. Strip me to her as you stripped me to myself. Tell Julia all, so she may know how the crooked deal came out and with it the lies, the whole rotten lies we were all living.

JULIA

(*Confused*)

Something crooked!

KENT

Yes. You'll have to know, Julia. I'll spare details now, but the fact is there. I want the decks cleared between you and me, and between me and myself.

DORA

No, no; Julia, he's exaggerating. He didn't do anything dishonest. He was merely forced to consider it— was tempted. It was *my* fault; my extravagances. We needed money——

KENT

Bah! I don't want that defense!

DORA

(*Forcibly*)

But you didn't do anything wrong, did you? You didn't do it.

KENT

(*Bitterly*)

Thanks to you, I didn't.

JULIA

(*Who has listened spellbound and is slowly grasping situation*)

You stopped him, Dora? And it all came out?

DORA

(*Quickly*)

We talked it over as you will all the common prob-
lems and difficulties when you are married.   This
mustn't come between you as it did between us.   That's
all.

KENT

(*Emphatically and with sincerity*)

That's not all.   I was going crooked, slipping into
the very class of men it is my business to put behind
the bars.   I was weak, wabbly, and a coward; afraid
to face myself with the truth till she toppled over our
life together to make me see it.   That's what I *was*.
(DORA *watches him with joy at his change*) But I've
got hold of myself in time.   I must prove to myself by
work and accomplishment that I did not need a
woman's sacrifice.   I must clean the rot and rust out
of my life; my insincerities, self-deceptions, hypocrisies
—all.   I must build an honest foundation.   I must
take life by the throat and make it give me what I need.
That's what I came to tell you, Julia; not to talk of
love.

DORA

Don't be the fool you said I was.   Don't cheat yourself and Julia by waiting.   I'm not in the way now.
I've done, finished.   Julia, tell him you want him to
stay.

JULIA

(*Impulsively*)

Not till he also knows all the truth about Fred.
Then he may choose.

DORA

(*Frantically*)

Julia!   Julia!

JULIA

Maybe he won't want *me* when he knows.

KENT

(*Not understanding*)

Won't have you?

DORA

Julia, you'll spoil everything.

JULIA

Maybe he won't want me when he knows I tried to
separate you, and failed—failed. Wallace, Dora does-
n't love Fred. She's sent him away forever. She'll
never marry him; she's going through divorce only for
us! She'll be alone, alone——

KENT

Dora, alone!

JULIA

(*Detecting the note of pity in his voice*)
You pity her, too!

KENT

(*In spite of himself*)
Why didn't you tell me that?

DORA

(*Defiantly*)
Why should I tell *you?* Why do you give me pity
when you refused to accept mine? Is that your idea
of *me?* Is that all you think *I* need? Can't I also
stand alone, as you said you could have? Do you
expect me to take your pity proudly and let it cheat
love? Is that the sort of woman you think I am?
It's you who are now insulting me.

JULIA

(*As she sees* KENT *stands spellbound eyeing* DORA)
She loves you, Wallace. She loves you.

DORA

(*Desperately*)
After what he said? No! No!

JULIA

Yes, yes! You want him to be happy above all
things. That's love. You're breaking your heart to

do it.   Let's have the whole truth.   Then he may
choose.

KENT

Dora?

JULIA

You love him.   I see now you've always loved him.

DORA

(*Fiercely*)

Well, what if it were true?   What if I were breaking my heart?   What if I do love him?

KENT

Dora!

DORA

(*Bitterly to* JULIA)

What has that to do with *you?*

JULIA

(*Shuddering*)

I can't think of his leaving you alone now.   I can't.

DORA

(*Fervently throughout*)

Why not?   Why not?   Can't you take him on that
basis?

JULIA

Oh!

DORA

It was easy to believe love was everything until you had to make the choice. You blamed me for sending Fred away, but you hesitate to take your love and you deny Wallace the rights of his love. (JULIA *tries to stop her throughout*) You called me a coward because I was true to what I thought was right when I felt there was something more in marriage than the mere passion that comes and goes and which we can't control. You thought I should have gone to Fred and left my husband, only because you wanted him. I tell you there is nothing in the way now of his leaving me. You can go with him, and if you will not take what life has offered you, I will ask which of us two is the greater *coward!*

KENT

Dora, listen!

DORA

(*Turning to* KENT)

And you pity me now; *you* who also blamed me, and burned your words in my soul so I can never forget them. You also thought all the years together were as nothing; that only passion counted; not the hours we had served each other in sickness, not the joys and sorrows we had in common, not all that I shared and sacrificed to make your career possible. They meant nothing, because you couldn't understand the difference between a theory of life and what actually was. You swept all away since I wounded your pride by telling you another man had caught for a moment my imagination when we were careless and unwatchful; and yet because I continued to live with you, and thought you had the greater claim, you called me *wanton*.

JULIA

(*Sinking in chair and covering her face*)
Oh!

KENT

Dora, for God's sake, stop!

DORA

Yes, wanton! Because I took your pretty things, your food and lodging and gave myself in return. Yes, those were your very words. You measured me and what I gave by the standards of street women; you forgot what I was willing to give to you; forgot I was faithful, forgot everything.—I tried to keep all this back, but now you know all the facts; everything is unravelled; there are no secrets. Throw me aside now, Wallace, as Julia thought I should have thrown you aside. Take her, as you said I should have taken my 'poor weak fool.' I've done everything I could to give you your chance for happiness together, as you said you would have given me. Don't do as I did: sacrifice and pity; or Julia will despise you as she always has me in her heart for what I chose. Do everything from now on as you both thought *I* should have done when I faced the same situation you now face. I'll never interfere with whatever you choose to take of life together before I am free.   Take everything! (*Slowly*) If you can.—If you can!

>   (*She goes out, closing the doors.   Then* JULIA *and* WALLACE *turn and gaze at each other in question.*)

CURTAIN

THE FOURTH ACT

THE FOURTH ACT

The same as the First Act. . . . A morning ten days later.

The room is now dismantled and everything is ready to be moved out. Barrels, boxes, and packing-baskets have taken the place of the furniture. The window-curtains, through which DORA *has gazed so often in all the varying moods of her marriage, are down—even the brass-poles and brackets have been removed; nothing veils the view to the clear skies without. Faint oblong shadows, where once the pictures hung, are seen upon the cold and distant walls. Those who had known the room would sense the subtle atmosphere of protest which inevitably comes with the wrenching of material things from their human relationship. It is only the silver loving-cup, upon the piano, which seems to have escaped the desecrating hand. No longer does one view a home; it is just a place where people still linger. Yet, somehow, it is a symbol; a visible statement of what happens in the universal rhythms of life, where only through the breaking-up of the old can one move on to new adjustments.*

DORA *enters, simply dressed. There is quiet sadness in her manner cloaked by an obstinate resolve. She looks about as though recording the new desolation; but controls herself. Then she goes to the folding-doors, which, as she opens them, expose the other*

room in the same condition, with some packers, super-
intended by WOODS, *methodically finishing their task.*

DORA

Woods. (*He comes down, closing the doors again*)
Is everything packed?

WOODS

They begin moving out shortly.

DORA

I hope they've been careful.

WOODS

They know people may use the furniture again in
time.

DORA
(*Evasively*)

We're only going to store it over the summer. Has
Mr. Kent 'phoned?

WOODS

No, Mrs. Kent.

DORA
(*Protecting him*)

He's fortunate to miss this.

WOODS

I've seen to everything myself.

Dora

You've been very good and faithful. You know I'd have been lost without you.

Woods

(*Venturing*)

One learns a lot about people in ten years.

Dora

Ten years! So it is.—I'm sorry to lose you.

Woods

My profession is not a permanent one.

Dora

I wish we could have made it so. Mr. Porter says he will place you; so you will lose nothing.

Woods

Thank you.   (*Significantly*) And your room upstairs?

Dora

We'll leave that till the last. Mr. Kent would wish it.

Woods

(*Looking about*)

It isn't easy to move after ten years; so much rubbish collects in a house; one never suspects how it gets there.

DORA

Yes; lots of rubbish.

WOODS

It's only when we tear up we really know what we have and what we haven't.

DORA

That's true, Woods.

WOODS

I beg your pardon—(*She turns*)—but I did not know whether you'd wish that loving-cup packed. I remembered your wedding anniversary comes next week.

> (*She looks at it standing forlornly on the piano. He glances at her and she is silent. He bows and goes out. It has seemed as though, for a moment, they had met and subtly understood each other.*
>
> *She moves toward the loving-cup, puts her hand on it half-affectionately and full of implication. Then she shrugs her shoulders, trying to shake off the memories it recalls.*
>
> PORTER *enters. He is very cheerful on the surface but there is an underlying strain of the situation.*)

DORA

Tom, I'm glad you've come. I was lonely.

PORTER

Everything ready?

DORA

Almost.

PORTER

That's good. I've been busy getting matters in order for you. (*He sits on a box, and takes a lot of papers out of pocket*) I went first to the Trust Company and find you can have your income sent you in monthly installments instead of semi-annually.

DORA

That's better. (*Smiling*) Now, I'll be poor only a few weeks each month.

PORTER

Then I went to the lawyers'.

DORA

You didn't——?

PORTER

Mention any names? Oh, no. So I suppose they thought I was in love with a married woman.

DORA

Imagine you.

PORTER

I was once—but only once. It's a troublesome luxury.—I find you'll need to go West; rent a house or a
flat. Stay six months. Of course, you can travel
while you're staying there. It's all here. (*Leaves
papers on box*) You can read them later.

DORA

(*Wistfully*)

How do I get there?

PORTER

Got the time-tables. (*Takes out four colored time-
tables which he also leaves upon box*) Four routes;
take whichever color looks prettiest.

DORA

(*Absently*)

I've never been so far alone before. (*Pauses*)
What about this house?

PORTER

That's all fixed. Quite unexpectedly got somebody
to sub-let it and turn it into a store.

DORA

(*Half shuddering*)

What kind of a store?

PORTER

Women's garments; you know, with lace on the pretty things that aren't seen.

DORA

(*With a faint, ironical smile*)

Pretty things? I wish it had been something else. —You have looked after everything, Tom.

PORTER

Had to, since you threatened to do it yourself. (*Absently*) You never will learn.

DORA

(*Hopelessly*)

Won't I?

PORTER

(*Affectionately*)

Not as an expert, I mean. But just call on me.

DORA

How can I always do that?

PORTER

I haven't anybody now myself and——

DORA

(*Affectionately*)

You're a little friend of the whole world.

PORTER

Truck and nonsense. Dora, this has sort of knocked me out, too. But I like to keep busy. I'm lonely myself, at times. But one's never *too* lonely if he's working for the happiness of what lies nearest. So I'm not doing this only for you; but for her also. *She'd* wish it.

DORA

Julia is a fine woman.

PORTER

How she and Wallace! (*With a sigh*) Well, no wonder she wouldn't marry an old duffer like me. (*She takes his hand affectionately*) So, little girl, we've got to help each other, you and I. We're left behind. They're not going to see sad, weepy faces if they look back, are they? We're going to buck up and show them we're game. I'll have you to look after, if you'll let me be 'just around the corner.' That's what Julia said. But she doesn't need me and you do a bit, eh? Guess I need somebody to look after, too. No sad faces, eh? We're game, eh?

DORA

It hurts, doesn't it?

PORTER

I've had pleasanter sensations.

DORA

But you think I've done right?

PORTER

(*Slowly*)

Whoever knows what is right? The answer always lies so many years ahead.

DORA

That's so, Tom. Yet there are many people who are always ready to blame and judge others. They forget every one marries to be happy, but no one can ever tell what the future holds. (*Smiles faintly*) I'm beginning to think husbands and wives should have a lot of sympathy for each other when things go wrong; but most of them have only bitterness. And I'm like the rest.

PORTER

If I only could get that patent to steer love right! Here we all are. We're pretty decent people—at least, we all had good intentions. Yet look how love has tangled us all up, and not one of us really at fault.

DORA

I thought I was somebody of importance to both Fred and Wallace. I was mistaken. Each would have been what he is without me. Yet I must have hindered Wallace instead of helping him.

PORTER

Nonsense, Dora.

DORA

Why, look how dependent I am even on you. It's easy to say you can live alone and all that. It's so different when you're suddenly face to face with yourself. I never realized before how absolutely helpless I was about these practical matters. Wallace always tended to everything. (*Almost shyly*) I've felt so lost these last days. I miss his being around. I'd grown so used to turning to him. I haven't shed a tear, but I catch my breath when I realize I've got to be all alone now.—What is it, Tom, that makes me feel so all alone?

PORTER

Let's call it habit, my dear; the habit of ten years.

DORA

I've been hunting the word; habit, that's it.

PORTER

It's stronger than love sometimes and gains its purpose just as effectively.

(WOODS *enters.*)

WOODS

Mr. Deering is here.

DORA

(*Assents and* WOODS *goes out*)

I promised Armor he should have some of the cut glass and——

PORTER

Funny where Julia is. Perhaps he knows.

DORA

(*Betraying nothing*)

Perhaps.

PORTER

Another of her sudden impulses, I suppose: to take a wild motor trip at this time.

DORA

(*Probing*)

You've not heard from her?

PORTER

I've received a half-dozen postal cards mailed from different parts of the state.

DORA

(*Puzzled*)

Different parts of——?

PORTER

Suppose she wishes me to get used to the postal-card habit. When's Wallace coming back from Rosemoor?

DORA

I don't know.   I've told no one where he is. · He
hasn't 'phoned.

> (DORA *is apparently puzzled.*   ARMOR DEER-
> ING *comes in, very cheerful.   They exchange
> greetings.*)

DEERING

(*Looking about room*)

Whew!

DORA

I'll show you what I have.

DEERING

I came ahead; I'm on my way down to the steamer.
Can't I look over the things later?

PORTER

Steamer?

DORA

It won't take a moment.

PORTER

Which steamer?

DEERING

Julia's, of course.   (PORTER *and* DORA *exchange
glances*) Yes.   Julia blew in on me last night.
Threw her arms around me and wept.   And then

said she was sailing at noon. I thought her trip was
all up, motoring more than a'week before she started;
so I went around with her. She hasn't packed a
blessed thing; said she'd forgotten it. Guess it's some
more temperament.

PORTER

(*Thoughtfully*)

So she *is* sailing.

DEERING

(*Surprised*)

Didn't she tell you?

PORTER

Got the days mixed.

DORA

(*Going up*)

If you'll come now.

DEERING

Sure I'm not stealing from you?

DORA

Not at all.

(*She is seen in back among things.*)

DEERING

Don't know how we're going to live up to our wedding presents on my income.

PORTER

You've done those Railroad fellows, eh?

DEERING

Yes. When they saw the evidence I had, they had to agree to plead guilty in a lower degree.

PORTER

(*Enthusiastically*)

And all on your own hook, too.

DEERING

I can't understand Mr. Kent not appearing.

PORTER

Wished you to get the limelight.

DEERING

(*Modestly*)

It isn't good for a young man's eyes.

PORTER

Give me your hand.

DEERING

It's been hammered to pieces nailing their lies.

PORTER

It's only the beginning with you, my boy. (*Affectionately*) Go straight!

DEERING

I must: to show Mr. Kent how much I appreciate what he's done for me. When will he be back?

PORTER

When this moving is over.

DEERING

(*Looking about*)

Say, moving must be——

PORTER

It is.

DORA

(*In back*)

Armor!

DEERING

(*Smiling*)

Ought to get married, Mr. Porter, really you ought.
(DEERING *goes up with* DORA *and then they pass out of vision.*)

PORTER

Can't understand why everybody wants to marry the bachelors off. (*Looks about the room*) Too bad! After ten years.

> (KENT *enters quietly. He is worn. He looks about and controls himself.* PORTER *turns; they see each other; he pulls the door to and comes down.*)

Dora has told me.

KENT

Then there's nothing to be said.

PORTER

Between men who love the same woman?

KENT

Fire away.

PORTER

It's not much. I'm the outsider. But the devotion of years may claim the right to ask something of you.

KENT

Anything, of course, Tom.

PORTER

Make and keep Julia happy; else, don't do it, don't! She is a woman in a thousand. She'll demand a lot. Be sure you have it to give.

KENT

(*He turns away enigmatically*)

And Dora?

PORTER

I'll always look after her.

KENT

(*Moved*)

Tom, I haven't been decent to you.

PORTER

(*Whimsically*)

How could you be when you thought Julia loved me?

KENT

(*Referring to room*)

And all this?

PORTER

Dora couldn't have done this alone.

KENT

It was not your place.

PORTER

(*With gentle reproach*)

That's what I thought; but you were at Rosemoor.

KENT

I was trying to solve a problem.

PORTER

Dora has worked out hers.

KENT

She hasn't a regret?

PORTER

She hasn't shed a tear—that we've seen.

KENT

(*Noticing time-tables*)

She's going West?

PORTER

Immediately. You'll see that your end is done. Accept service and better be represented by counsel. Saves future complications if there ever should be children.

KENT

Children! (*As though to himself*) I wonder how it would have been if Dora and I had——? (*He puts the thought aside*) She's going to take that trip alone?

PORTER

Got word to-day that some mining interests would need my attention for six or seven months, so I thought—— (KENT *puts his hands impulsively on*

PORTER's *shoulders in thanks*) Don't thank me. I've got a deal on that will clear up a small fortune.

KENT

Money! That's so. They've finished me, haven't they?

PORTER

Done up brown.

KENT

Without a crust, eh?

PORTER

Well, quite by accident a little bit flew off in the baking. (KENT *questions*) I suspected trouble; so I got Biddle to let me in at a low price. I believe your brokers managed to save a few thousand for you. They'll keep silent, too. It will help you turn around. And, Wallace, I believe there's a chance for a little capital in this copper deal I'm——

KENT

(*With determination*)

No, Tom. I pay off every cent here: her debts and mine with what I can make in practice. Then I begin clean.

PORTER

So law's cleaner than copper, eh?

KENT

The first step is to get this over.   It's almost incredible, after ten years.

PORTER
(*Quickly*)

Don't look back; memories are nasty things to bring a second wife.

KENT

What makes you say that?

PORTER

I never had one of those luxuries, but I know Julia.

KENT

Strange; you should say that, too.   (*He turns*) Where's Dora?

PORTER

With Armor; he stopped on the way to see Julia off. (*Closer*) Do it decently.

KENT
(*Evasively*)

I want to see Dora.   I'll wait till we are alone.

PORTER
(*Puzzled*)

But what are your plans?

KENT

I'll tell you later.

PORTER

(*Taking his hand*)

What's the trouble?

KENT

I'm suffering, Tom.
(KENT *controls himself and goes off quickly*
towards the library.)

PORTER

Not happy with Julia in reach! The men are just
as hard to understand as the women.
(DEERING *re-enters, opening doors and talking*
cheerfully. WOODS *passes in back of them and*
goes to the main door. DORA *also comes*
down.)

DEERING

What's the matter, Mr. Porter?

PORTER

Matter? Nothing. Don't ask any questions but
when you get off by yourself will you swear for me?

DEERING

Certainly; I will now.

(WOODS *re-enters.*)

WOODS

Miss Deering.

DEERING

(*Looks at watch*)

I've got to hustle.
> (JULIA *enters, dressed for traveling. She, too,
> is halted by the appearance of the room. Her
> manner throughout is calm and firm in contrast
> to the previous act.* WOODS *goes off in back,
> closing doors.* DORA *watches* JULIA.)

JULIA

You're going to see me off, Tom?

PORTER

One of the specialties I do best.

JULIA

(*Looking at* DORA *slowly*)

I've come to see Dora alone.

DEERING

I'll go look after the trunks.

PORTER

I'll go along with you.

DEERING

Do. Blew myself to a cab. See you later, Mrs. Kent.

(*He goes off.* JULIA *detains* TOM; DORA *looks out of window.*)

JULIA

Tom, I've written you a long letter. (*Takes it from her pocket-book and gives it to him*) Will you read it to-night?

PORTER

(*Moved*)

I've always waited to be alone to read your letters.

JULIA

This one will explain.

PORTER

You need explain nothing. The world is full of people who are left behind.

JULIA

But you see I haven't quite forgotten the Rock of Ages.

PORTER

May I add some flowers to your luggage?

JULIA

No, no. No flowers now. (*Smiling sadly*) It will never be good-bye between you and me. Just give me a handshake and some strength—for a little while.

PORTER

Maybe I need all I have of that. I'm too old a dog to hope for myself. (*Whimsically*) I—I hope *you* will be very happy.

JULIA

' Quietly happy,' you said. Yes, I shall be that in time, Tom.

PORTER

I'll be back, Dora. Rock of Ages! Hump! Guess I'll incorporate myself and sell shares!

> (*He goes out quickly, trying to conceal his emotion. The two women face each other. The following played very quietly.*)

DORA

Julia, you're sailing alone?

JULIA

Yes, alone.

DORA

It's best that Wallace sail later, of course.

JULIA

He won't follow me.

DORA

Then you find you don't love him enough?

JULIA

It isn't that.

DORA

But, Wallace?

JULIA

I have tried to make him understand.

DORA

I don't. Does he?

JULIA

Men see some facts slowly.

DORA

It's because of me?

JULIA

Yes.

DORA
(*Firmly*)

It is useless.

JULIA

That cannot alter me.

DORA

He knows my part in his life is finished.

JULIA

Except what has been between you.

DORA

Ah! You feel that, too. (*Poignantly*) Isn't it in my power to give him happiness even through stepping aside?

JULIA

Can a mere word cut you out of his life?

DORA

You fill his heart.

JULIA

Do I? A heart is such a little thing. It's I who wish him happiness, more than anything else in the world.

DORA

Away from you?

JULIA

It could not be together. He may have a chance otherwise.

DORA

(*Firmly*)

He must live alone.

JULIA

Better that than what would happen to me. I've learned much about myself and this problem of marriage in the hour since we three were together. I have gained a clear insight into what I must do.

DORA

Which is?

JULIA
(*Firmly*)

To leave him.

DORA

(*Slowly*)

How calmly you say that.

JULIA

There has been and will be enough of the other thing.

DORA

And this is Julia Deering!

JULIA

The *real* Julia.

DORA

You're sacrificing the man you love uselessly.

JULIA

No; if I were to marry him you'd be in the room watching. You would always be between us. He would never be entirely mine. You belong to one another.

DORA

By what right—now?

JULIA

By the right of ten long years.

DORA

(*Repeating*)

Ten long years.

JULIA

Listen, Dora. Because he was unattainable he filled my thoughts; yet when he came to me I saw clearly what all the years of thought unconsciously had done. They had bound you to him in my eyes; always the thought of him had been also the thought of you, because you two were man and wife and I was the outsider.

DORA

Not that, Julia, if he loved you.

JULIA

To think of Julia Deering ever seeing that passion, after all, is only crisis—all crisis; but that the habit of living together becomes a state of mind.

DORA

(Half to herself)

Habit! Tom said——

JULIA

Dora, I've lived with the *thought* of Wallace but you have lived with the man. You said it all that day in a few words. You've shared the daily habit of living; you've walked beside him; he's held your hand; you've eaten at the same table; moved in the same room; sat by each other's bed in illness and shared the hidden intimacies while I lay in the night alone. And then his work. I could never be part of that. It isn't my sort. This all means something more than what he and I may have felt for each other.

DORA

But aren't you big enough to forget all this?

JULIA

It isn't my jealousy that makes it impossible between Wallace and me. It's what you unconsciously made me realize: that there's a bond between you two; the bond of most nowaday marriages. It's not made by passion nor even complete understanding; but by *habit,*

habit: that mechanical, ordinary, day-to-day, bond of marriage.

DORA

The daily habit of living! I thought only those who were married knew how strong that is.

JULIA

I know it—*now*.

DORA

So you have come to see that marriage is just walking along the road together—if the comrade is kind and understands a little.

JULIA

Yes.

DORA

But we did not understand each other at all. So it's impossible between Wallace and me.

JULIA

Other women might honestly have solved it differently. I'm only telling why *I'm* going away.

DORA

Too bad, Julia; for I am leaving him, too.

JULIA

Think it over.

DORA

I have—after what he called me. (*Shuddering*)
Oh, it shames me every time I think of it.

JULIA

You are obstinate.

DORA

It's what some women have in place of strength.
(*Half scornfully*) Did he send you to plead with me
to live with him again?

JULIA

I don't believe even he would ask that.

DORA

Then he does understand me—a little.

JULIA

Good-bye now. I must go while I am still as I am.

DORA

I called you weak. (*Goes to her*) Julia! Forgive
me. I don't blame you. All we can do is what we
see is right.

JULIA

(*Drawing back*)

No, don't kiss me, Dora.

DORA

(*Keenly*)

I ask no questions about these ten days.

JULIA

You would not believe any answer I gave.

DORA

No; for I know, if necessary, a woman would always lie about some matters.

> (JULIA *turns as* WALLACE KENT *enters with a letter in hand. He is surprised at seeing* JULIA.)

JULIA

No words, Wallace. Good-bye. I'll never regret unless you fail to take life by the throat. Good-bye, Dora. Remember me a little, Wallace, as one who will be ' quietly happy.'

> (JULIA *goes out, hastily controlling herself.* KENT *sits down with head bowed.*)

DORA

At least *your* memory will be worthy. I'm sorry, Wallace.

> (*She goes and puts her hands sympathetically on his shoulder. Her eye falls on the letter.*)

KENT

My letter of resignation. It was not mailed?

DORA

No. I thought it might be merely an impulse. Besides it wasn't right for you to retire at this time when that Railroad case was——

KENT

You thought of that?

DORA

Your term has only a few months more to run. Finish it; it will protect you from criticism in the future.

KENT

It was good of you.

DORA

I felt once this career was partly *mine;* I did not like to see you throw it away uselessly because two women touched your life.

KENT

I suppose the strongest men brush women aside.

DORA

The strongest men *should* when woman's emotions interfere.

KENT

This sha'n't hurt me. Work, not sentiment, is the normal man's life.

Dora

I'm so glad you see that. You'll get hold of yourself now. I've been the hindrance; my dependence must
have dragged you back. You will soon be free of me.

Kent
(*Looking at her*)
But where will you go after——?

Dora

I haven't looked so far ahead.

Kent

You must.

Dora

I'm thinking first what's best for you; and after
what you said that day, I know.

Kent

I was cruel.

Dora
(*With deep conviction*)
No, you were right. It *was* an insult for me to
stay merely because I feared you'd go to pieces. But I
saw it that way at the time.

Kent

Dora, I understand better now. Before you leave
I hope you'll forget what I said.

DORA

We are both learning to understand each other at the end. It might have been better had there been truth between us.

(WOODS *enters.*)

WOODS

Pardon me, Mr. Kent, but the men——

KENT

What men?

DORA

The movers. Better let them begin in the other room, Woods. (WOODS *goes out*) Tom thought it best to put everything in storage first; it will save comment. I've given the china and glasses to Armor. There are some things to divide. We must go over them.

KENT

Now?

DORA

They are mostly upstairs. The linen and all that sort I have given to Woods. Your books are packed separately. You'll direct where to send them. (*Takes loving-cup from piano*) Woods came across this cup your fraternity gave us when we were married. (*Half smiling*) I don't know who owns it.

KENT

(*Reading inscription*)

" To Wallace Kent and Dora Houston, with all best wishes for your happiness."—This will be the first time in ten years we've not drunk a toast on our anniversary.

DORA

What foolish sentiments one has at the beginning.

KENT

How can you talk like that?

DORA

Because it seems to symbolize the irony of our marriage.

KENT

No; the habit and community of interests.
(*The men are heard passing off back with furniture as* KENT *stands looking at cup.* DORA *has crossed and speaks off.*)

DORA

Be careful, don't scratch that table. (*Turning*) What difference does it make? (*She sees him sitting there*) Put it away, Wallace. It's over.

KENT

Dora, for God's sake, don't.

DORA

It's not easy, Wallace; but it must be gone through with.

KENT

Must it? Dora, I couldn't get away from the thought of your living alone.

DORA

You must.

KENT

But it's not Tom's place to help you; it's mine, if you'll let me.

DORA

All you can do is to make it easier for me now.

KENT

Dora, we've only got each other. We're both alone.

DORA

Yes, alone. (*Controlling herself*) But let's look it in the face. It's good-bye, Wallace, good-bye. We're saying good-bye here in this house we've lived in for ten years. Don't let's look back——

KENT

But all life is looking back, Dora. Is this necessary now? What do we gain by living apart? What victory do we bring ourselves?

DORA

We test our strength and——

KENT

But we are two human beings, Dora. And that means we are both strength and weakness.

DORA

I'm thinking of you, Wallace. I can be of no further use to you.

KENT

But there is much you can give me. Isn't there something I can give you? Haven't we learned to understand each other through all this? Dora, we've been kind to each other as people go; we've got along somehow; we have more than most people. Isn't there something sweet and noble we can still give each other?

DORA

Would you want me to give everything as before?

KENT

Live in the same house with me—if nothing else.

DORA

No, Wallace. That's impossible. We are a man and a woman. Don't let's fool ourselves as we did each other.

KENT

I can't demand. You have the right to go and if you feel it is for your good, go. I'll not hinder you. But I wish you'd stay and go along with me—together.

DORA

To walk along the road together?

KENT

Yes. That's what I ask. Won't you?

DORA

(*Thoughtfully*)

And this is marriage!

KENT

As *we* have worked it out.

DORA

I thought it could have been something greater!

KENT

So did I; but it lay only in what *we* were.

DORA

Yes, that's it; and what we are. (*With a look of hope*) And what we can still make it. Wallace, I do feel helpless by myself; I am afraid of the loneliness. My heart goes out to you because of what we've had. My heart perhaps is waiting for yours——

KENT

You will stay?

DORA

Yes, if——

KENT

If?

DORA

If you just let me cry. I want so to cry.

(*She bows her head. He puts his hand upon her, as she sobs quietly. He soothes her tenderly. The bright sunlight floods the dismantled room.*)

CURTAIN

www.ingramcontent.com/pod-product-compliance
Lightning Source LLC
Chambersburg PA
CBHW050529260626
47157CB00004B/1524